Books by Alexa Milne

The Call of Home

Choosing Home

Returning Home

Lust Bites

Stay

Single Titles

Sporting Chance
Not Every Time
Comfort Zone
A Bell Rings

Returning Home

ISBN # 978-1-78686-001-9

©Copyright Alexa Milne 2016

Cover Art by Posh Gosh ©Copyright 2016

Interior text design by Claire Siemaszkiewicz

Pride Publishing

Published in 2016 by Pride Publishing, Newland House, The Point, Weaver Road, Lincoln, LN6 3QN, United Kingdom.

Pride Publishing is a subsidiary of Totally Entwined Group Limited.

The Call of Home

RETURNING HOME

ALEXA MILNE

Dedication

Thanks to the usual suspects for the help and advice given as I pulled my hair out trying to write this story.

Chapter One

Darach McNaughton peered through his windscreen at the snow falling in thick flakes around him. The window of his sister's café appeared dark and unwelcoming.

He grumbled to himself. "Where the hell is she?" He fished in his pocket for his phone. "Damn!"

Another place with no signal. He'd have to change providers, if he could find one that worked. Maggie would know. Once more he wondered why he'd chosen to come back to the Northeast Coast of Scotland. This didn't happen in Glasgow. And, oh yes, he'd returned to the back of beyond because of his most recent case and because of his bastard of a cheating boyfriend.

He squinted at the window again, attempting to see if there was a light under the kitchen door – nope. Maybe the weather had made her decide to go home early. Darach thought about his home – the farm he'd grown up on with his parents, brother and sister. Other than his brother, they would all be there waiting for him, his family, staring at him with questioning eyes, speculating as to why he'd turned down a promotion in Glasgow to come back to his home town. He couldn't tell them. He couldn't tell them about the final straw, of the dead woman beaten to death by her violent husband while her child had watched, or how useless he'd felt at being unable to prevent it from happening. How she'd gone back time and time again like a moth to a flame, despite the help he'd offered her. Yet another victim he'd been unable to save. He couldn't deal with it anymore. He'd had twelve years on the force in Glasgow and had spent the majority of them with Mitch, the boyfriend he'd found in bed with someone else the day he'd come home early after finding Jenny's body. He'd offered his resignation from the force, but his boss, Gina McKinnley, had suggested the transfer. He'd left Glasgow and that cheating bastard behind him.

He climbed out of the four-wheel-drive Skoda he'd splashed his cash on — glad he had with the current weather conditions — and trudged through the now settling snow to the door. The note stuck there simply said, *GONE HOME*. Well, that answered his question. A loud plaintiff meow interrupted his thoughts. Turning, he saw a large brown cat walking up and down on the wall behind him, snowflakes sticking to its fur.

"Stupid puss. Why aren't you home in front of a roaring fire in weather like this?" He didn't like leaving the animal as it continued to meow at him.

"I don't speak cat." He brushed the flakes from the animal's head and it nudged his palm.

"Here, Princess. Here puss." The voice sounded as if it was coming from behind the end house.

"Is that you? You look like a princess with your beautiful collar. Let's see if you have a name on your tag." He reached and pulled her studded pink collar around. The heart-shaped tag declared her name.

"So you are Princess, and it sounds like your owner is trying to find you." He picked her up and clutched her to his chest. She showed no signs of objecting to him. "Looks like I'm taking you home."

The voice still echoed from along the road. A single-story house stood at the northern end of the linear village, which was basically one street, separated from his sister's café by a small car park and a playground. One somewhat ineffective street lamp illuminated his way as he trudged the one hundred yards or so to the house. The front door was shut, but he could see a light from within. The shouting continued, so Darach opened the gate and made his way down the path between the garage and the house to the back. When he turned the corner, light flooded onto the snow-covered garden from the open door.

"She's here," he shouted in warning of his presence. "I found her down the street and thought I'd bring her when I heard you calling." He stopped at the sight of the young man sitting in a wheelchair at the back door. Princess struggled in his arms and he let her go. She jumped down and scampered past her owner and into the house.

The young man in front of him certainly didn't fit the image of the person he'd been expecting. Darach guessed he was in his early twenties. His bleached blond hair was shaved at the sides but longer on top. Thin and pale, he wore only a long T-shirt with tattered jeans. His arms and neck displayed tattoos, which Darach imagined continued over the rest of his body. He stared, taking in the sight of him until his brain finally switched on.

"You'd better get inside. It's bloody cold out here and you're not exactly dressed for this weather. Are you all right? Do you need anything?"

The young man scowled at him.

Shit! Now I sound like a patronizing git. Just because he's in a wheelchair doesn't make him useless.

"I'm fine. Thank you for bringing Princess. She does have a habit of roaming and picking up strangers."

Darach held out his hand. "I'm Darach McNaughton."

The cat's owner didn't take his hand or give his name. Darach shifted uneasily and pushed his hand back into his pocket.

"She's a beautiful cat and huge as well," he said, knowing he should have been gone by now, but somehow not wanting to leave.

"She's a Norwegian Forest cat. They grow big and are perfectly at home in the snow. I need to go back in now. You're right, it is cold. Thank you for bringing her." He wheeled his chair back, ready to close the door.

"Right then, I'll see you around."

"Maybe."

The door closed, and Darach heard the man speaking, no doubt admonishing the cat. He brushed the snow from his coat and made his way back to his car.

The track to his childhood home, with its fresh covering of snow, provided a bumpy ride in the dark. Eventually, he turned a corner and the farm appeared out of the gloom, its lights showing through the blizzard conditions. To the side of the main house, now the residence of his sister, brother-in-law and nephew, lay several outbuildings and the newly constructed bungalow where his parents now lived. The front door opened as he pulled up the handbrake. His sister, Maggie, stood framed in the doorway. He grabbed his overnight bag from the seat and climbed out of the car. Sprinting, he wasted no time getting to the door and out of the snow blowing around him. Dogs barked in the background.

"Get in here," his sister said, stepping back. "You saw the note, then."

Darach removed his coat and shook it out at the door before turning around to hug Maggie tightly. "Yeah, I saw it." He hung the coat on one of the hooks and brushed his jeans off, sending snow down onto the large mat. Two dogs rushed at him until Maggie shouted, and the border collies sat obediently awaiting further instructions.

"You look well, sis."

"Unlike you. Are you sleeping?"

He knew she was right. He had bags and dark circles under his eyes from lack of sleep. At least he had a week until he started work to sort out his new house and get settled in. Currently, it had the appearance of a slightly organized bombsite. Boxes were stacked on top of each other, but most remained unopened except for those containing such immediate necessities as a kettle and toaster. He'd have to buy new furniture. Currently, he was sleeping on a sofa he'd had delivered from a catalog, and it was none too comfortable. Mitch had claimed much of what they'd shared because he'd kept the tenement flat they'd owned between them. Splitting everything up had led to more arguments about who owned what, until he'd simply given in, not wanting to argue anymore. He would find time to go bed shopping and buy the biggest one available.

"I'm fine, honestly. I need to get a new bed, that's all. Unsurprisingly, I decided to leave the last one with Mitch, seeing as I caught him screwing someone in it. I assume they're all here."

Maggie patted his arm and he swallowed his temper down.

"Yep. Couldn't keep them away. Are you ready to face everyone? I've told them not to ask questions about Mitch, but I had to fill them in with the bare details." He'd told Maggie what had happened between him and his ex, despite the hurt and embarrassment. Even though they'd lived apart for twelve years and she was five years older than him, they'd remained close. Their eldest sibling now lived in Australia, but Darach wouldn't have been surprised to find out they'd organized a call on Skype to unite them all.

"Better face the music, then."

Four expectant faces greeted him when he entered the main room. Somehow this was different from the visits he'd made twice a year—this was permanent. Now he would be able to see them all the time, be able to drop in, when his job allowed, and they'd be able to visit him too. He'd have time to babysit Bobby and take him out to places like a good uncle should. As if he'd read his mind, the six-year-old jumped up from the floor and wrapped his arms around Darach's legs. Darach picked him up and swung him around as much as he dared, conscious of the ornaments and photo frames crammed along the mantel.

"Uncle Dar, Uncle Dar. Did you see the snow? Can we go out tomorrow on the sledges? Can we? Daddy says he'll be too busy, but you're not working yet, are you? Mummy said you weren't, so can we?"

9

"I guess so, if you've been good."

Two brown eyes fringed by long lashes stared up at him when he placed him back carefully on the floor. "I'm always good." Bobby glanced over at his mother who hummed loudly. "Well, nearly always. I only hit Kurt because he was mean to Xander. He's always mean *and* he's a bully. I bet you'll have to arrest him when he's older, Uncle Dar. Can Xander come over tomorrow?"

"If he can get out and his parents say it's okay." Bobby and Xander had been born on the same day six years before and had been inseparable ever since. He had a sudden memory of him and Tosh when they were so young, running around the farm, getting into mischief, building dens. He supposed he'd see him around with his new husband. He wasn't sure if his postal rounds would extend to Darach's new house on the coast road.

His parents rose from the sofa and Darach hugged them both. His father, as strong and as vital as he'd ever been, still worked the farm he'd inherited from his father. His mother, a farmer's daughter herself, had been one of the local vets until her recent retirement, but still kept her hand in, tending the stock on the farm when she could and when her health allowed. He loved them both, and they'd accepted him without question, even losing friends when he and Tosh had come out and Tosh's parents had initially told their only son to leave their house. Of course, Darach's parents had taken him in, and Tosh had remained close to them after their split and his decamping to Glasgow.

"*Tsk*, you've not been taking care of yourself, son," his mother whispered in his ear. "I bet you haven't been eating properly. You're too thin for a start. Good job your father made one of his stews. Good Aberdeen Angus steak with veg and dumplings — it'll line your stomach and help fatten you up again."

He smiled. There was no point arguing with his mother,

and his father did make great stew. His brother-in-law greeted him, arm outstretched.

"Good to see you again, Darach. Are you sure you've time to take him out? You'll have boxes to open, no doubt."

Darach grasped his hand and shook it. "It'll be fine, Rob. I like spending time with him, and you'll have things around the farm you could be doing with him out from under your feet."

"There certainly are, but now it's time to eat, so everyone at the table."

It was like old times, all of them talking over each other, memories of Christmases past and of winters with snow covering the ground. Being on the coast, they didn't get as much snow as inland when the air was pushed up the mountains, but when they did, it could stick around for weeks—no fun with livestock to care for, especially if the weather took a turn for the worse in lambing season. He recalled many occasions on which the whole family had been out searching for ewes caught in snow drifts. His mind wandered back to the young man with the cat.

"I met your neighbor and his cat when I was outside the café," he said. "He seems an unlikely person to find living in a small Scottish village. Is there a story?"

Maggie gazed at him, eyebrows raised. "He arrived about two years ago, but we still don't know much about him. Keeps himself to himself and says very little. The cat likes to visit the café, though, and charms the visitors. He's an artist and makes the most wonderful pieces of pottery and decorated tiles, but remains something of a mystery."

"Does the mystery have a name?"

"Yes, his name is Brice Drummond."

Chapter Two

Brice Drummond, interesting name. Somehow it didn't sound real. Who the hell was called Brice? But then again, there weren't many people with his name, either. Darach couldn't resist a mystery, especially when wrapped around someone as striking as Brice. He mused for a while on how he could manufacture a reason to see him again, until Maggie nudged him in his ribs.

"Penny for them," his sister whispered in his ear.

"Sorry, just thinking."

"And I can guess what about. Harry at Actual Antiques might know more. He stocks Brice's paintings."

"He paints as well?" It just showed you shouldn't judge a book by its rather glorious and unusual cover.

"Landscapes—I told you he has talent. He also designs tiles for Davy Kerr to go in his kitchens. Rob was in school with him and with Ellis McKenzie, his doctor, but *he* definitely won't tell you anything."

Darach chuckled. "I'd forgotten how small this place was. Everyone does know everyone, don't they?"

"Oh, and Tosh is his postman."

"How is he?" The pit filled with guilt opened up in his stomach again.

"Happy. You should have come to the wedding. He missed you."

"I couldn't. I'd recently split up with Mitch and had the flat to sort out. I couldn't face seeing my first boyfriend all happy at getting married. I had hoped he'd understand."

"He understood, exactly like he did when you split up in the first place. You had different priorities, that's all. You wanted to see more of the world than he did."

"At least he didn't go all the way to New Zealand." His mother interrupted their conversation. "I don't know why your brother had to go so far away to find himself."

His father leaned over and touched his mother's arm. "Gray's happy over there, Peggy, with his wife and their sheep station, and at least we can Skype."

"I miss him, though, and we might never meet our grandchild when it arrives."

Darach's mother had begun to show signs of losing her memory. Maggie had tried to persuade her to get tested, but she'd resisted so far. It was only a matter of time before she would be forced to face the truth. Signs of dementia when she wasn't quite seventy promised nothing good.

"We all miss him, Mum," his sister replied. She was always the person who tried to reconcile everyone.

Darach made an effort to change the subject. "Hmm, I knew I'd missed something being away for so long. Dad, this stew tastes incredible. The beef is melting on my tongue."

His father opened his mouth to speak, but Darach beat him to it. "Please don't tell me what the animal was called. You know I hate it when I'm eating one with a name."

Every adult glanced up from their food and sniggered at him. Darach threw up his hands in mock protest. "Oh, for Pete's sake… You lot… I can't believe my own family…and in front of Bobby as well."

Bobby glanced around, puzzled. "What?" he said in between mouthfuls. "Does this meat come from one of our cattle?"

"Don't worry, Bobby. Your uncle is trying to be funny." Maggie glared at him then burst into laughter again

Darach couldn't stop himself and joined in. Still, at least they could joke about his sexuality. Coming out hadn't been a problem. They'd been more disappointed when he'd given up on university and joined the police force.

"You always were a complete wimp when the animals

had to be slaughtered."

Maggie was right, of course. He'd toyed with being a vegetarian as a teenager, but it hadn't stuck. Now he was one of those people happy to eat meat as long as he didn't have to face where it came from, which had been a lot easier in Glasgow. There, he didn't have to be up close and personal with the source of his bacon sandwich.

"I know I'm a hypocrite."

His father snorted. "You and the rest of the population. Farming isn't a job for the faint of heart. At least one of my children has carried on the family tradition. We've been here for so long holding out against the big companies."

Now it was his mother's turn to interfere. "Stuart, there's no point in having a go at him, and you didn't want this life to begin with either. You used to talk about seeing the world when we were young."

His father put a hand on his wife's arm. "I made my decision, love, and I've never regretted it, staying here, marrying you, even having this annoying brood."

Darach's mother rose from her seat. "Let's have ice cream. Would you like some, Bobby?"

"Yes please, Granny. Can I have sauce on it?"

"Of course, your granddad will want chocolate and strawberry on his."

By ten, everyone other than his sister had gone to bed. Darach had walked his parents through the snow to their cottage and made the decision to stay rather than drive home in the dark. Rob had milking in the morning so had gone up already. He and Maggie nursed tumblers of whiskey and stared at the flickering firelight.

"Are you really all right?" she asked.

Darach examined the whiskey for a few moments before answering. "Not yet, but I will be. Too many bad things happened all at the same time. I had a case, a young mother, beaten to death by her boyfriend. I'd tried to help her, to persuade her to leave, but she couldn't. She had nowhere to go, she said. Her mother was dead and her father an alcoholic. There are so many families on estates, so many drug dealers ready to provide, too many loan sharks willing to take their pound of flesh. When I came into the job, I had this idea I'd be helping people, and now I wonder if I've helped anyone at all. Mitch fucking the guy he picked up in a club, in our flat, in our bed, was the last straw. He said I wasn't fun anymore, and perhaps he was right. Mitch somehow managed to shut off from the bad stuff, and his patch in Edinburgh, for all its beauty, has huge social problems just like Glasgow. If Mitch wanted to forget, he'd go dancing, get wasted, and find a young piece of arse willing to bend over for him. This one was simply another guy. He definitely wasn't the first. Mitch took joy in explaining in great detail what they gave him and I didn't."

"At least you had the sense to walk away after you forgave him the last time."

"I intended to leave the force as well, but Gina, my boss, told me they wanted a sergeant at Buckie. She thought working here might be less demanding than Glasgow. So here I am, all alone and back home, having to start again." He swallowed the rest of the whiskey and poured himself another—as he wasn't going anywhere. Washed up at thirty, his dreams of career success and finding love all vanished. He had a right to feel sorry for himself, didn't he?

Maggie sat up in her armchair. "This bloke, Brice Drummond, he interests you, doesn't he? I've seen that expression on your face before. He's been in the shop, usually to rescue his cat, or if he's run out of something he didn't have delivered, but he doesn't talk much. He manages his wheelchair along the pavement all right and goes down the main street to the local shops. Princess likes to sneak in here and curl up on the windowsill. Our regulars don't care, but some visitors don't like having her around. She's a little beggar and loves our bacon and cheese."

"She's a beautiful cat, though. You said he makes pottery and paints?"

"Harry stocks his pottery—all in rainbow designs and

patterns. He makes tiles for Davy to go in bespoke kitchens and fireplaces. So many people have wood burners in hearths these days, and the tiles are simply beautiful. Those are his."

Darach glanced at the green tiles with a yellow buttercup design. They were stunning. "Do you know how he ended up in a wheelchair?"

"Nope. He appeared here around two years ago. He doesn't get any visitors, as far as I've seen. His accent suggests Edinburgh. He told us this area was better for his craft and for inspiration. He has an adapted car, so I guess he goes out and sketches. Sometimes he's away overnight."

Darach smiled.

"What? You said it was a small place, and it is. It won't take long for everyone to know you're back in town."

Darach didn't suppose it would, especially once he started work again. His thoughts turned back to Brice. "His tattoos, from those I could see, were floral as well. He had a strand of ivy winding around his neck and down one arm." He sighed. "Probably best I stay away. The last thing I need to do is get involved with someone, especially someone like him, even if he's interested in a washed out, out of condition policeman. I still can't help wondering what he ran away from, because there was fear in his eyes when he saw me—fear and defiance." He didn't mention the slight flicker of interest he'd also seen in those pale blue eyes as the man had peered out from under long blond lashes edged with dark eyeliner, or the way Darach's cock had wanted to find out more too. Maybe the guy had too much physical damage to—be interested. He couldn't imagine how it would feel—not to feel—not to be able to.

"What?"

"I was speculating about the extent of his condition."

Maggie raised her eyebrows. "Whether he can still get it up, you mean?"

Heat rushed into his cheeks, not caused by the whiskey. "Is it wrong? Maybe I shouldn't even be thinking about him in that way. Or is it wrong not to think he's fanciable because of his condition? Jeez, I need to get my priorities sorted."

Maggie leaned closer. "As it happens, I can help you with that particular question."

"Pardon?" He stared at his sister.

"Our cleaner, Janet, works for him as well. She said she found lube and other things in a box under the bed when she was hoovering. Usually the box is locked, but he must have forgotten and she couldn't resist peeking. I told her not to mention it to anyone else. So maybe it's only his legs that don't work."

Darach shook his head. "Nah, I won't have to see him again unless he breaks the law. I have to concentrate on getting the house sorted, then we've Christmas and I've a new job. Now I need to get some shut-eye, if I can manage to sleep on this sofa."

Maggie rose from her seat. "It's probably as comfortable as the one in your house. I'll get you a couple of pillows and a duvet. The fire is banked up for the night."

Later, he pulled the bedding around him and closed his eyes. In his mind, he painted a trail of ivy down and around the mystery man's body until it reached his arse, or his cock, leaf pointing downward. His cock stiffened in his briefs. "Not here," he murmured before tiredness overtook his desire.

Chapter Three

The next week passed by in a blur of Christmas activity and unpacking. On his first day of work, Darach changed into his uniform in the station locker room, used as he was to not to wearing it to work, and brushed his shoes. He wanted to look his best before he met the inspector and the rest of the small team. The snow had been replaced by rain, but at least it meant the main roads were clear. He took a deep breath and made his way to the open plan office area. Each station in this part of Scotland had a small team led by an inspector. Darach rapped on the glass door and followed the instruction to come in.

The man who greeted him with a smile and an outstretched hand had the reddest hair Darach had ever seen and freckles covering most of his face. He shook the proffered hand.

"Sergeant Darach McNaughton, sir, reporting for duty."

"Good to see you, Sergeant. I understand you're a local man."

"Yes, sir. My parents own a livestock farm."

"You'll find it a little different around here from Glasgow, but we have our usual suspects and our targets to achieve like everywhere else. We need to justify keeping these stations open, and keep the public and the powers that be happy. I've teamed you with Constable Carmichael over there. He's young and keen and he knows everyone. He's good with the local youth as well, and he's our liaison with the schools."

Darach knew both the local primary and secondary schools were next to the station. "That'll be useful, sir. My nephew attends the primary school, so I'll be able to drop him off and pick him up at times."

"Right, so I'll take you through and Gus can fill you in on any outstanding cases then take you for a spin around the area, even if you are local."

"It's been twelve years since I lived here, sir. I'm sure many things have changed. I'm eager to get stuck in, though, and make a difference." And he was. Having time with the family had been fun, but he needed something to keep his brain occupied. He glanced over at the young man sat at the desk in the corner and hoped they'd get on. Coppers needed to know their colleagues had their backs. There had been a few who had made the odd comment about his sexuality, or given him an odd glance, but outright abuse could cost them their job these days, so most kept their negative opinions to themselves.

Gus Carmichael raised his head, met his gaze and smiled — a good sign. "I'll get on with it, then, sir."

Darach closed the door behind him and strode across the room to where the PC stood waiting to greet him. They shook hands and sat down to have the same conversation about being local. Gus, short for Angus, was one of five brothers from Findochty. Darach realized he knew his family, being especially familiar with his brother, Sam.

"I remember you from school," Gus said. "You wouldn't have noticed me."

Darach was somewhat surprised to discover Sam had returned home after university and was now a Church of Scotland minister. Gus filled him in on the local issues, drugs, petty theft, rural crime, antisocial behavior, and road and public safety.

"You're here in time for Hogmanay tomorrow. We don't usually have too many problems beyond the odd case of drunk and disorderly, but people have been known to get violent, or they drink and drive. We'll be about keeping an eye on things in all the usual places. And now I'll take you out and show you the best place to get something to eat."

Gus drove him around the area. Once again, Darach

was reminded of the beautiful place in which he had been brought up. Both countryside and coastal villages, even in the gloom of a wet winter day when every building appeared gray, all revealed something glorious. The landscape was bigger, less closed in, the roads clearer, the air cleaner, if rather refreshing. The sea smelled differently here as well. Gus filled him in on the variety of local characters and places, the drug sellers, the bars that might have problems and the difficult families as they made their way in and out of the small coastal towns, finally arriving in a familiar place exactly at one o'clock.

"And this place has the best food in the area," Gus declared, pulling up outside Maggie's café. "They use only local produce, and the steak and onion baguettes are to die for. It's this place that means I have to hit the gym a few times a week."

Darach couldn't help but smile as he followed Gus through the door. Maggie raised her head and grinned back at him then approached their window table, notebook in hand.

"Who brought who?" she asked. Gus looked confused for a moment then hit his forehead with his palm.

"Of course, you two know each other."

"Maggie is my sister," Darach explained. "Gus is a big fan of yours."

"Not so much mine," she said, nodding to Melanie, her assistant. She bent over. "Ask her out. She's interested. I asked her."

"Really?" Gus sighed, blushing furiously. "Think she'd like to go to a party with me?"

"You won't know unless you ask. Whose party?"

"My best friend, Jason's. It's his birthday, and a housewarming as well for him and Davy." Those names couldn't be merely a coincidence.

"Davy Kerr?"

"Yeah, that's him. Do you know him?"

Darach shrugged and glanced at Maggie before answering.

"Not well. Davy went to school with my elder brother," he explained. "You know what it's like here. He turned back to Maggie. "We'll have two steak and onion baguettes with chips and two hot chocolates, Mags. And you go and ask the girl out, Gus. She keeps glancing over here."

Once Gus had followed his sister to the counter, Darach turned his attention to the window. Curled up in the corner lay a familiar furry creature. He reached out and rubbed her ears. "You're a real beauty, aren't you? And you know it. Why aren't you in with your daddy?"

"She doesn't like being shut in the house by herself when I'm working." He turned around to see Brice Drummond.

"How? I didn't see you come in. Some policeman I am."

"There's a side door with a ramp because of the step. And I have to keep her out of the workshop or she gets between the paint and what I'm painting and ends up covered in specks. I sometimes forget the time, so she pops out through the cat flap and ends up here."

"My sister said you were a potter and an artist. I thought I might check out your work in the shop down the road."

"Maggie's your sister?"

"Guilty as charged," Maggie said, putting the food down on the table.

"How's he doing?" Darach asked.

"Mel fancies the pants off him, so it's a dead cert she'll go. I see you two have met. Can I get you lunch, Brice? Princess has been treated to smoked salmon already."

"No, thanks. I had a sudden craving for buttered toast. Do you have any walnut bread? I won't stay. I've pots in the kiln. It's interesting to meet you again…" He stared at Darach's shoulder. "Sergeant McNaughton."

Maggie brought Brice the wrapped-up loaf and Brice wheeled himself out of the café. Princess jumped from the sill and meowed at the door. He stood and let her out, watching as she followed her owner down the road. When he turned around, Gus had already started to consume his food with obvious enthusiasm.

"Mel agreed, then?" Darach asked.

Gus nodded and licked at the sauce escaping from the corner of his mouth. They ate without talking, allowing Darach time to consider the man he'd tried hard to get out of his mind over the last week.

"He's a bit of a strange fish," Gus said when he'd finished his food. "All those tattoos and the shaved head. Jase says he's all right, though. He's invited him to the party."

"Is he going?" Darach asked. "Maggie said he keeps to himself."

"Jase wouldn't take no for an answer. Their house is all on one level out toward Portgordan, so he couldn't use the excuse that it wasn't accessible for his chair. They've done such a great job on it and have used Drummond's tiles and paintings. Why don't you come as well?"

"I might be working."

Gus winked at him. "I'll sort it if you are. I did a few favors for people over Christmas, and we're working tomorrow, so I think I can swing the night off for both of us at the weekend. You can reacquaint yourself with a few people and maybe meet some new ones."

"Will Jason mind if a stranger turns up?"

"You're not a stranger, and he won't care. Anyway, I'm sure Maggie and Rob will be there."

"Then I'll take you up on your kind offer." And he'd have the chance to talk to Brice.

"We'd better get going again. We've quite a few farms to visit who want us to give them security advice. We've had a spate of machinery thefts and that stuff isn't cheap, as you know. It gets dark early this time of the year, so I don't want to go down those still-slushy lanes and take out a tire."

On his way back to the car, Darach glanced down the street to Brice's house, glad that the world wasn't such a big place.

* * * *

Brice watched the police car go past then wheeled himself to his kitchen to make the toast he'd wanted earlier. Princess jumped up onto the work surface and sat watching him. How did cats always manage *that* look? She fixed him with a sullen glare, which spoke of her superior intelligence and that she knew something Darach didn't. She should have been sitting there filing her nails nonchalantly, not rolling her eyes at him.

"What?" Brice asked, putting the slices of bread in the toaster. "It's your bloody fault he came here, so don't you dare put on your innocent and butter-wouldn't-melt face. All right, I might have flirted with him slightly, but you did as well, I bet. I imagine you lay on your back, showing off your gorgeousness. At least I haven't done that yet."

Princess gazed at him again and mewed softly. "So, are you saying I should go or not? A little flirting would make a nice change. I'm not fucking dead yet, despite everything." His cock had definitely suggested it remained alive and open to suggestions.

"I know I'm supposed to keep myself to myself, but it's been two years, and it's only a party. It's not like I'm going to pull someone at a housewarming, is it? No one in their right mind would consider me to be boyfriend material."

The toast popped up and he spread butter over the surface until it melted into the bread. He opened his mouth, took a mouthful and chewed, letting the melted butter coat his tongue.

"This is so good. Maybe next time I'll make French toast."

Princess head-butted his hand and meowed at him. He put a small dab of butter on his finger and let her lick it off.

"You are such a spoiled girl. I know you had smoked salmon earlier, so don't think I'm going to feed you again until later. And no more matchmaking. I know what you're like. Anyone would think you were worried about me being lonely or something."

The cat lay on the worktop and rolled around on her back. "I'm not falling for that, young lady. Three strokes of your belly and I'd have every single one of your claws buried in my flesh." Princess mewed at him again.

"All right, I agree he's easy on the eye, and I'd bet he bats for my side, despite the uniform, but there's no reason to imagine he'd be interested in me. Maybe it would be good to join the human race again for a while, but I've too much to hide, Princess. And no bloody truncheon jokes from you either. I'm not into that stuff anymore. Let's face it, I'm not into anything anymore, except my flesh-light friend, which is as near as I'm going to get to a willing arse being stuck in this thing."

Brice ate the second piece of toast then wheeled himself to his desk. Taking out his sketch pad, he closed his eyes to recall the image he needed, then he began to draw. Princess jumped up and watched him create the image in charcoal. A few strokes of the pencil and a few minutes were all Brice needed to capture Darach's features perfectly. "Fuck! This won't do, Princess. I don't want to be thinking about him—not now." He put the pad face down. "So what will I wear to the party, then? Gay or straight, male or female, or a little of both? Makeup or no makeup? Maybe a little eyeliner rather than the full-on shadow and lipstick." Was North-East Scotland ready for gender bending? Somehow he doubted it. Jeans, T-shirt and a cardigan, then. He could rock a cardigan, especially the pale blue one that matched his eyes. The timer rang, letting him know his pots were ready.

"Now, you stay here, Princess, and let me work without worrying where you've disappeared to this time. Then I won't have to deal with you bringing strange men home again." Princess raised her tail and pranced off to the bedroom. He smiled, knowing that without her he'd have gone mad and risked everything by returning to Glasgow. She'd kept him safe, as well as keeping him sane.

"Come on, work to do." He opened the back door and maneuvered himself down the shallow ramp and path to his workshop.

Chapter Four

Half an hour into the party and Brice began to wonder if he'd made a mistake bothering to come at all. After he'd spent a few minutes talking to Jason on his arrival, the host had left him to his own devices and, since Brice didn't know anyone else, he wheeled himself into a corner and sipped his one bottle of beer. Sometimes he missed the drugs. For years, he'd swallowed practically everything he'd been offered — coke, uppers, downers, poppers — but he'd never injected, no matter how many times he'd been offered the stuff. The addicts had come time and time again, desperate for their fixes, and he'd determined never to be like them. Now he was clean, thanks to an extended stay in the hospital and an urgent need to accept that it was time to grow up and fend for himself in the chair.

Although he hadn't believed it at the time, he did have something to live for now, even if it was only a cat and his craft. He glanced up from his beer and locked gazes with Darach McNaughton. Usually, when he stared for long enough, the other person turned away, embarrassed, but the policeman held his gaze. Brice knew a challenge when he saw it, and he deliberately reached down to adjust his pants, gratified to see those darkened eyes follow his movement. When their gazes met again, Brice grinned. Okay, maybe he was playing with fire, but this guy was a cop and surely, if anyone was safe, a cop would be such a person. He imagined his sixteen-year-old self ever trusting a policeman and laughed. Where he came from, the boys in blue were the enemy, to be avoided at all costs. He hadn't trusted them before his sister and…

"Thought I'd come and join you in the corner." Brice heard the scrape of a chair next to him. "I don't know many people here, either. I like the T-shirt, by the way."

Now he was next to him, Brice could see the image adorning Darach's top. "Agent Coulson — interesting choice. Most people would have chosen a superhero."

"Or a villain like Loki." Darach nodded to the image on Brice's chest. "What do our choices say about us, do you think?"

Brice pushed his fringe back then pulled down the hem of his T-shirt to expose the picture. "In my case, it shows I fancy bad boys, or maybe I'm a bad boy myself. So are you a good guy like Coulson, trying to protect the world?"

"I *am* a policeman."

"But there's more to you than your job, isn't there? Everyone ought to let their hair down sometimes."

Darach's eyes widened and his pupils expanded as he shifted on his seat. He opened his mouth to say something but was interrupted.

"There you are."

Brice pulled his gaze away to see a man and a woman standing over them. He recognized Mel from the café and the younger policeman who'd come in with Darach a few days before.

"You decided to come, then?" Gus continued.

Brice wasn't sure which of them was being addressed. He fixed a smile on his face.

"We haven't met properly. My name is Gus and I work with Darach. Jason is my best friend. He said he'd asked you to come." He held out a hand and Brice shook it briefly. Gus scanned the room. "They've done such a great job with the house. I love the tiles in the kitchen. Jason said that you designed them."

Brice nodded. "The tartan patterns were a bugger to get right, but what Davy wants, Davy gets. I did the thistles around the fireplace as well."

"Well," Mel continued, "people are talking about your

work, so you might get more business out of this evening."

Another man appeared behind Gus, and Darach stiffened beside him.

"Darach, it's been a while."

Brice glanced sideways as Darach held out his hand.

"Yes, about twelve years. I should have joined the dots and realized Gus was your brother. You came back as well then." A woman appeared at the blond man's side before he could answer.

"This is Emma, my girlfriend. Emma, this is Darach. We were in school together and... I'm sorry, I don't know your name," he said, addressing Brice.

He held out a hand. "I'm Brice Drummond." He caught the glimpses between this man and Darach. There was a story there. "I'm sorry, I don't know *your* name."

"Sam Carmichael, one of Gus' brothers."

"He has four," Darach explained.

Gus put his arm through Mel's. "We'd better get to the kitchen and get some food or it'll all be gone. It was good to meet you again." Brice watched the four of them amble toward the kitchen.

"So what's the story with Sam?" he asked, gratified to see Darach's cheeks flush.

"Let's put it this way—I'm surprised to find out he has a girlfriend."

"Ah—well, people can change or extend their appetites."

"Talking of appetites, d'you want something to eat? I don't mean to insult you, but things are getting rather crowded, and you might find it hard to maneuver your chair through the masses."

Usually, Brice would have gone without, or insisted he could manage, but instead, he nodded. "Thanks—a few nibbles would be good. I lost track of time working this afternoon and skipped lunch. I'm a vegetarian so no meat or fish. Anything else will be fine."

"You can't afford to skip meals." Darach's facial expression showed concern, and Brice's cheeks warmed with embarrassment. No one had been concerned about him in many years—perhaps never.

"I'm fine," he protested.

"You could do with putting on a few pounds and getting some color into your cheeks."

"Not much chance of getting a tan up here. The summer isn't exactly reliable, and getting outside can be an issue. People tend to stare at the freak in the wheelchair with the tattoos and strange hair. You stared at me."

"Perhaps not everyone has the same reason for giving you the once-over."

Brice shivered and gripped the arms of his chair. His cock hardened in his skinny jeans, pressing against the zipper. He needed to get his body under control. He tried to swallow, but his mouth had gone dry and he coughed. Darach handed him a bottle.

"It's only Coke," he said. "I don't drink."

Brice swallowed several mouthfuls, conscious of Darach gazing at his throat. His cock stiffened further as desire surged through his body. He wanted Darach's lips on his neck. It had been so long—so very long—since another person had touched him. He stopped swallowing and stared. The air between them crackled as the rest of the room disappeared. This situation between them, whatever it was, had spiraled out of control. Brice breathed out and regrouped. "Thanks, and the food you mentioned would be good."

Darach rose from his seat and put a hand on his shoulder. "I'll be a couple of minutes. Don't go anywhere."

He glanced back on his way to the kitchen, but Brice hadn't turned to follow him. Darach had watched him for ten minutes before he'd made his presence obvious. He'd chatted to Jason and Davy with Maggie and Robbie when they'd arrived and, unsurprisingly, Maggie had mentioned Brice. Darach had been impressed by the tiles, but the painting above the fireplace in the main room had caught his attention more, and he noted Brice hadn't even mentioned that he'd created it. It showed the house with the sea and sky as a backdrop at sunset. Pink, blue and orange bled into each other in the watercolor. The man had talent, that much was obvious.

As he made his way to the food spread out on one of the kitchen surfaces, Darach couldn't help but think there was something familiar about Brice. His mind returned to the ivy tattoo just visible above the neckline of Brice's T-shirt, but there could be any number of reasons why it might be familiar.

"So did you find out anything about your mystery man, then?" Maggie stood selecting food when he arrived.

"Not much except he's an Avengers fan and he likes to flirt. I get the feeling he's testing me."

"Well, as I said, no one has any gossip or any information about why he decided to come here. Even Davy and Jase have no idea how he ended up in the wheelchair. They've never seen him out of it, so I guess whatever happened to him is permanent."

"Maybe he's always been in the chair. It could be something he was born with," Darach replied. "Does it matter why he's in it?" He grabbed two plates and began to put a selection of sandwiches and other party food on each. Maggie smirked at him.

"What?" he asked. "So I'm getting something for him. You're getting food for Rob, aren't you? It would be difficult for him to get through here. I have discovered he's a vegetarian, but I imagine you know that already."

He felt the weight of a hand on his shoulder.

"Hello, Darach."

He turned to see his first love standing behind him next to an older man. Tosh hadn't changed much. He imagined walking miles every day on his rounds kept him fit. His hair had begun to recede, but those blue eyes were still as distracting.

"Tosh, it's good to see you." He wasn't sure what to do,

but Tosh made the choice for him.

"Put those down a minute so I can give you a hug—it's been too long."

Darach did as he was told and found himself pulled into Tosh's embrace while the other man looked on. He breathed in a familiar smell—Tosh still used the same aftershave. He pulled out of the hug.

"This is Harry, my husband," Tosh said.

Darach reached out his hand to the tall, thin man at Tosh's side.

"I'm informed you own an antique shop," Darach said to make conversation.

"That's right. It's on the same road as your sister's café. The village has gained quite a reputation for its crafts as well as the antiques, so we get lots of visitors. I do well enough, and I sell local craft products as well. People like to get original works as holiday souvenirs. Tosh tells me you're a policeman."

"Guilty as charged," Darach replied as Harry scrutinized him over half-moon glasses.

"I can't help but think you're going to find it much less interesting around here than in the big city." Anyone who had eyes and ears could have worked out this man wasn't thrilled with his return—not to mention the territorial way his arm rested around Tosh's waist. Darach wanted to let him know he was no threat to their relationship. He picked up the plates.

"I'd better get these back to Brice, or he'll think I've gotten lost."

"Oh, you're here with Brice, then," Harry said.

Tosh's eyes widened at the information as well.

"Not exactly," Darach replied. "We've met a few times and I said I'd get him some sandwiches."

"I'm surprised he let you. He's kept himself to himself since he arrived in the village. I've stocked his work for over a year, and he's very sellable, but he's not been exactly forthcoming. I know nothing of his past, or why he moved here. He is rather beautiful, though, isn't he? Sometimes there's such an air of fragility about him — and not simply because he's in a chair. He has such sad eyes. But he's such a private person. Maybe you can get him to open up. Tosh thinks you both deserve a little fun, and everyone should have someone to love, don't you think?"

Darach wasn't sure how to reply. Harry had wrapped his arm around Tosh's shoulder during his last words. He guessed Tosh had told him about his split with Mitch, and his friend at least had the good grace to look embarrassed.

"You and I should have a boys' night in sometime and catch up," he said deliberately gazing at Tosh. He couldn't help himself. "We could get drunk and reminisce about old times."

Tosh appeared uncertain for a moment then smiled as Harry tightened his grip, pulling him closer. "Ignore him — he's trying to wind you up exactly like you were him, and as wonderful as it is to have two strong men butting antlers over me, I'd prefer it if you both stopped, unless you want to go the whole hog and get your dicks out to see whose is bigger. If my memory serves, there's not much in it."

Maggie guffawed and turned it into a cough. "I'll take this to Rob. No sister wants to hear a conversation concerning the size of her brother's dick. Play nice, all right? That's all I ask. I'll let Brice know you're on your way."

Darach noticed Harry's grip on Tosh had loosened. Harry held out his hand. "I'm sorry, Let's start again, shall we?" he said. "I'm being a jealous pillock. Sometimes I can't believe I managed to persuade him to marry me."

Darach shook the outstretched hand. "You've nothing to worry about, Harry. One gander at the way this idiot stares at you like he wants to lick you all over tells me everything I need to know."

Both men blushed and glanced at each other.

"See? You're both doing it now. I'll leave you to it."

Harry put a hand on his arm. "I meant it about Brice. There is an air of sadness around him. Maybe you can get under his protective shield and find out more."

"I'm sure Tosh has told you I've recently finished one relationship. I don't intend to get involved with anyone."

"Maybe you both need a friend, then. He has a story to tell."

Darach wound his way through the people to where Brice waited, conscious of how long he'd been away. "I'm sorry," he said, handing over the plate and fork. "I met an old friend and his new husband, and we had a difficult conversation—you know the one, I'm sure, when you meet your ex-boyfriend for the first time." He sat on the chair once more and popped a mini quiche in his mouth.

"I can't say I've ever introduced a new boyfriend to my ex," Brice replied.

"Sorry, I wasn't implying anything by using the word boyfriend. I don't know if Maggie mentioned I'm gay. I don't suppose it's likely to have come up in conversation."

Brice shot him a glance and chuckled to himself. "No, Maggie hadn't mentioned you being gay. A gay policeman—my, times have changed from when pretty coppers used to entrap men in toilets."

"That was a long time ago now, as you well know," Darach said. "There's a gay group in the police these days. My ex-partner is an inspector in Edinburgh."

Brice straightened in his chair. Obviously something in what Darach had said had made him sit up and take notice. "Do you know Edinburgh?" Darach asked, hoping to discover something about the enigmatic man. "Maggie said you hadn't mentioned where you're from?"

"I've lived in a few places. My family moved around the country. Was your ex the reason you came back home? Maggie said you've been away quite a while."

"I left when I was eighteen, dropped out of university and joined the force in Glasgow. I was there twelve years and it was time for a change. I had to..."

"It's all right. You don't have to tell me." The softness of the tone Brice used threatened to overwhelm him. Tears pricked at his eyes. He stared at the floor and swallowed hard before attempting to move the conversation on to a more neutral topic.

"Jason and Davy said you painted the canvas above the fireplace—it's beautiful. I love the colors blending in the sunset. Have you always been creative? That must have been difficult if you moved around a lot as a child—you know, with schools and things."

"I've loved art since I was young enough to appreciate it. I used to go to museums and galleries on my own and stare at the exhibits until security threw me out. When I got home, I'd recreate them with crayons, or anything else I could find. School wasn't exactly my thing. I spent most lessons doodling when I actually went at all."

"Do you see your family anymore?" Darach asked.

"No, but we weren't exactly close."

Darach guessed there was a lot Brice wasn't saying, but he continued. He wanted to know more. "Did they disown you because you're gay?"

"I never told you I was gay," Brice snapped back. "And I don't have any family now, except for Princess."

Darach couldn't help but speculate about why. Had Brice been injured in an accident that had wiped out his family? He might be able to find something online. Brice Drummond couldn't be such a common name. Time to stop putting his size twelves in every conversation, back track and change the subject again.

"I'm sorry. I didn't mean to imply anything about your sexuality." He remembered something else Maggie had mentioned before, concerning Davy and Jason's neighbor down the coastal road. "Maggie said the house farther along belongs to Davy's uncle and his partner, the writer Richie MacNeill. I'm such a big fan of his books. Have you ever read them?"

"No, but I'll check them out if you recommend them."

"He writes crime stories. The lead character is a gay detective called Guy Boyet. They're set in the U.S. There's a

TV series as well and rumors of a film. I've all the boxsets. I'll bring them around for you."

"Thanks, that would be good. I don't watch much. With my work, I tend to get carried away and lose track of time then find it's the early hours of the morning."

They discussed films and TV for a while, both, Darach suspected, happy to be on a neutral subject rather than explaining themselves. After thirty minutes or so, Brice yawned. He did appear tired.

"I'm going to get off now," Brice said. "I didn't get much sleep last night. Sometimes I get pain and the tablets don't deal with it. I usually get up and paint then."

"Do you want help getting out of here? I don't want to offend you by suggesting you aren't capable of coping on your own."

Brice fixed him with a soft smile. "I guess I can be a bit prickly about the chair. People tend to assume my mind doesn't work either and talk slowly or shout at me. I've had to learn to fend for myself, but yes, a little help would make things easier if you could make a space in front of me to get to my car."

Darach did as he'd been asked and they made their way out to the driveway in front of the single-story house. He noted Brice's car to the right and helped by pushing the chair over the gravel. Brice lifted himself from the chair into the front seat then folded it, put it in the back seat and shut the door before winding down the window.

"It's specially adapted for me," Brice explained. "I guess I'll see you around if you're going to become a regular at the café."

"I guess you will, as Gus obviously has a thing for Melanie as well as my sister's cooking. It's been good—talking to you. I'll drop those DVDs around to you, and maybe we could go out sometime."

"Are you asking me out on a date?" Brice asked.

"Would you go if I was?"

"I don't know. I've never been asked out before."

"Really? I can't believe anyone as beautiful as you are hasn't ever been out on a date before."

"The chair puts a lot of people off, but not you, it would appear."

Darach smiled. "No, not me."

Brice turned the engine on. "Ask me again when we see each other. I'll think about it. I'm not promising anything."

"That's good enough for me. Take care driving home and give Princess an ear rub from me — she's a beauty as well."

Darach moved away as Brice maneuvered the car out onto the main road. He shivered in the cold winter wind then turned to go back into the warmth of the house.

Chapter Five

Despite the late hour and the likely reception he'd get from Princess for not coming into the house immediately when he arrived home, Brice wheeled himself into his workshop, set up his easel and pulled out a small canvas from the stack at the side. He didn't use oils much, but a portrait seemed to demand it. He squeezed half a dozen colors onto his palette and began mixing then applying the paint, working quickly. Darach's features weren't yet etched into his consciousness, so he closed his eyes every so often in order to remember each detail to form a whole. Darach's face had an ordinary shape with his skull slightly longer on the left-hand side — most people wouldn't even notice. His light brown hair was cut short, but not too short, with longer strands on the top. Brice guessed if Darach ever let it grow, the curls would win. It was kept out of his face by gel holding the length up and back. His forehead had depth and a few hints of lines with his eyebrows visible and slightly darker in color than his hair.

Brice sketched out the basic shape of Darach's face, planning out the features in the way he'd read about in library books he'd found, trying to get the proportions right so the eyes were in the correct place and not too high, the nose didn't dominate. Darach's nose was straight and narrow but not too long, except for a slight turn at the end. It wasn't anything you could describe as Roman or aquiline, simply a nose that fitted in his face with nostrils that might flare when annoyed or excited. His cheekbones were there, but hardly defined, and his mouth was neither big nor small, his bottom lip, wider than his top one, was definitely chewable. His only outstanding facial feature was the small dimple in his chin, which was round, not pointed or square. His eyes were simply blue—not cerulean like the sea on a bright day, or pale like a washed-out sky—just blue.

Once he'd finished putting everything together to form a whole, Brice knew he'd have to paint another because the face in front of him didn't show the real man or his major feature—his smile. Darach's smile transformed his face, making his eyes shine, giving him cheekbones and dimples and raising the corners of his mouth as he showed his teeth. Brice imagined what his face would look like in the throes of an orgasm, with his head back and his mouth open. Instantly, his cock responded to the visual in his mind. He had no idea why this man had such an effect on him. It had been more than two years since anyone had touched him and even then... No, he didn't want to go there, or remember those feelings, the longing, the need to be... He wheeled himself back, assessed the finished piece and yawned. He glanced at the clock. Time to sleep. Princess would no doubt be waiting for him, but would ignore him and accuse him of abandoning her. She'd walk around with her tail held high, not coming near enough for him to pet her until he'd been punished enough.

He opened the kitchen door and, sure enough, Princess watched him from the table without moving then, with a swish of her bushy tail, she jumped down and stalked off toward his bedroom. He watched her leave, locked up then wheeled himself down the corridor to the bathroom. The compensation for his injuries had allowed the single-story house to be redesigned to fit his requirements. He wanted a shower, but tiredness won over and he dragged his reluctant body to his bedroom. Princess had already settled and stared at him from the duvet.

"What?" he said. "You flirted with him, too, and don't deny it. You were practically on your back wanting him to tickle your tummy."

She yawned, stretched and turned around before settling

back down again.

Brice smiled. He caught sight of himself in the mirror. How long had it been since he'd smiled so many times in an evening? How long had it been since a handsome, not to mention sexy, man had paid attention to him without him worrying what might happen as a result? He undressed and grabbed the support hanging from the ceiling to lift himself into the bed. He reached out a hand and ran it through Princess' long coat. She purred happily under his touch. For a while, he stared at the ceiling. Darach was obviously interested in him and Darach was a copper, so he should be able to trust him. It had been two years now. Surely they couldn't expect him to live like a monk forever? Yes, he'd come to this godforsaken place after giving evidence for his own protection, but did that mean he had to be on his own forever?

* * * *

A few days later, Brice heard a knock. In the past, he'd have panicked, worried about who it might be and why they were there. He pressed a button on his laptop and the black and white image from the CCTV camera showed him Darach McNaughton, dressed in civvies, smiling at him. Brice wheeled himself to the front of the house, unlocked the door and opened it. Darach held up a bag.

"I come bearing gifts. And it's fucking brass monkeys out here so I'd appreciate coming in."

Only two people had ever stepped inside the house with him — his doctor, the grumpy Ellis McKenzie, and his cleaner. Brice wheeled back to allow Darach access before shutting the door.

"I bring food and the DVDs I promised," Darach said. "Maggie made vegetable soup today, and I have some of the crusty walnut bread you like and a really tangy lemon cheesecake. You could do with putting on a few pounds. Now...bowls, plates and cutlery?"

"Over there," Brice said, pointing to the cupboard before wheeling himself to the table. "The cutlery is in the drawer to the left of the sink."

Darach busied himself. He brought the bowls to the table, pulled out a large flask and poured the contents into two bowls. Brice had to admit it smelled glorious. He reached into the bag and grabbed the bread.

"Butter's in the fridge," he said.

Darach sat opposite him, tore off a chunk and dipped it into his soup. "Afternoon off," he said. "Been on nights. We've had a series of thefts from cars in supermarket car parks. We caught the bugger red-handed last night after setting up a sting."

"Must be a big change from Glasgow?" Brice said between mouthfuls. Princess jumped onto the other chair and rubbed her head against Darach's elbow before rolling around on her back. He reached out and rubbed her tummy. Brice counted under his breath—one, two, three—but she continued purring.

"You are a tart, cat. Usually she'd have bitten you by now. She likes exactly three seconds of belly rubs before she turns."

The smile Darach gave him changed his face, caused crinkles around his eyes and gave him dimples. "What can I say? It must be my natural charm for soothing savage beasts."

"Done a lot of savage beast soothing in your life, have you?" Brice asked. A vision from his past shot into his mind and he shuddered.

"You okay?" Darach asked, reaching over a hand and placing it on Brice's arm.

Brice snatched it away. "Someone walked over my grave," he said before taking another chunk of bread and using it to wipe the bowl clean. "This soup tastes so good. I love Maggie's soups, and she always makes a vegetarian choice. Her lentil is my favorite."

"I'll remember next time," Darach said. "I was

wondering… Would you show me your workshop? I need work done in my new house. I've bought a two up, two down on the coast road. It's not much, but it's mine and it has a better view than my flat in Glasgow had. I thought I might get the kitchen redone first. I like to cook and I loved the tiles that you did. Maybe you'd like to come for a meal and give it the once-over, or we could go out. I've heard the restaurant at the Lodge is good. My friend Tosh and his partner married there before Christmas. You know them. Tosh is your postman and Harry owns the antique shop along the road."

Brice gripped the arms of his chair and took a few breaths to try to control the panic clutching at his chest. It was true. He'd never been on a date with anyone, let alone someone like Darach who gave the impression of being straightforward and level-headed, and interested in more than the contents of his pants. Maybe he thought those contents were as useless as his legs. He struggled to get a handle on his emotions. "Yeah, I know them. They invited me to their wedding, but I didn't go. Sometimes it's hard, you know, on your own in places."

"Well, I hear the food is good. The ex-footballer Zac McKenzie owns it."

Brice shrugged. He hadn't played any sport, having been small and weedy in his teenage years, his only advantage being able to get out of tight spaces quickly when he had to.

"Not a football fan, then?" Darach asked.

"Sport was never my thing." He glanced down. "Which is just as well."

"How did it happen?" Darach asked.

Brice had been dreading this question. He had a story, of course. He couldn't tell what had actually happened, the names they'd used as they kicked him from head to foot, breaking bones and covering his body with bruises before they left him for dead.

"Car accident. Icy road – I hadn't long passed my test – lost the use of my legs after injuring my lower spine."

"That's tough when you're so young."

"Yeah." *Leave it at that.* "Why don't we eat our cheesecake first, then I'll show you the workshop. I've some tiles ready for the kiln. Maybe I'll show you how to throw a pot."

"Can we re-enact the scene from *Ghost*?" Darach asked.

Brice's cock twitched with interest at the thought of being enveloped in those strong arms, leaning back, having Darach's hot breath on his neck, pressing back against him.

"You're more likely to get covered in clay. But whatever you make, you can paint, and I'll fire it for you."

"Can't wait," Darach said, spooning cheesecake into his mouth in double-quick time.

Brice loved his workshop. In it, he lost track of time while he made beautiful things. For so much of his life, he'd been surrounded by dirt and poverty, the gray of the rabbit hutch-style flats he'd lived in matched by the gray of the sky on most days. Ugliness in all its forms had dominated his existence — people and things. Only the museums and galleries had saved him.

He opened the door of what was the separate garage. On one side, he kept supplies, paints, clay, glazes, varnishes, spare canvases. At the far end stood his kiln. He ought to get one with a bigger capacity, but he could wait for now. On the other side, he had a potter's wheel and his easel. Because of his wheelchair, there had to be enough room for him to move around and everything had to be meticulously organized.

"Wow, this place is fascinating," Darach said, closing the door behind him. "Can you show me how you make a pot?"

Brice grasped a dollop of clay and settled himself in front of his wheel, positioning his legs either side.

"You have to make sure you center the clay properly and keep the wheel turning. This wheel is especially made for people in chairs to use." He slammed down the clay and wrapped his hands around the piece. It helped having long fingers as he placed each hand, one at the side and one at the top, pushing down slowly.

"Keep your hands wet and apply pressure to the top while holding the sides until it's fixed in place."

"You make it seem so easy."

"I've had lots of practice. When I first started, the clay went everywhere, but I watched a lot of YouTube videos and learned more and more. I don't do anything clever with the shapes. Most of my fun comes from playing with the glazes and making different colors. Potting requires a good understanding of chemistry. It's not an exact science. That's why making the tiles can be hard, and why I only make them in small batches to scatter the patterns through plain colors. You can end up with mistakes, but people like to buy them as well. Every one of my pots are one off— unique pieces with individual decoration, mostly different sized bowls and vases. I'm still learning how to do more shapes, mixing glazes and creating new patterns. Now I'm going to make the vase with my fingers."

After a few minutes the simple vase had been shaped.

"I need to do the rim and finally it's ready to be removed with this." He picked up the wire with its wooden handles and slowly ran it underneath the pot as it moved around.

"And there you go," he said, picking it up with both hands and putting it to one side.

"I think this one would look good with a handle." He smiled to himself, knowing how the process of pulling a handle could affect people. He picked up another lump of clay and rolled it on the flat surface next to the wheel to create a long piece of clay. After wetting his hands, he held the length up and wrapped his fingers around it and began to pull slowly, fully aware of how it appeared.

"We call this pulling," he said, as he continued to stroke, gradually creating the right thickness.

"Really?" Darach swallowed then coughed.

"Yes, I find this motion so soothing."

Finally, happy with the effect he'd had on both the man and the clay, Brice attached the handle to the vase and sat back. "Then it gets glazed and fired and it's ready for use.

You'll have to let me know what colors you'd like."

Darach shivered then recovered his equilibrium. "My living room is green and cream and this will look wonderful on the windowsill, so something with those colors would be great."

"I'll check on the tiles in the kiln. They should be ready now." He wheeled himself forward and busied himself while Darach investigated the rest of the room.

"Oh, my God."

Shit! He'd forgotten the portrait still on the easel under the cover. Darach stood staring at it when Brice turned.

"You painted me. It's awesome. I didn't know you did people as well as landscapes. You'd make a fortune selling these. And you painted me from memory?"

Heat rushed into his face, but Brice was unable to stop his cheeks flushing red. "I've a good memory for faces," he said. "But I don't do many portraits."

"I'm honored, then. You've made me look good."

"It wasn't difficult to do," he said.

Darach closed the distance between them. Without thinking, Brice raised his face and stared into those blue eyes. Desire curled in his stomach. It had been so long.

Darach leaned over, turned his head to one side and kissed him. His lips were soft and warm. Brice wanted to put his hands behind Darach's head and pull him in, but he let Darach keep control, parting his lips enough to allow their tongues to meet, tentatively at first, until Brice opened his mouth and Darach pressed in, placing a hand on either side of Brice's face. He'd never been kissed like this—so sweetly and softly. Tommy had preferred other parts of his body, only occasionally offering any tenderness in what he did. Tears formed in the corners of his eyes. He needed to end this before his emotions overwhelmed him. He pulled away.

"Sorry," Darach said quietly. "I thought you wanted me to kiss you. I didn't mean..."

"No, don't apologize. It's just... It's been a while since

someone has kissed me."

"The world must be full of fools, then."

"What?" Brice said, unsure of the exact meaning of those words.

"Not wanting to kiss you."

"Oh." Bloody hell. He was acting like a virgin who'd never been touched, which was so far from the truth. Could he do this? Could he expose himself and his full catalogue of secrets? He stared at Darach, fending off a whimper at the concerned expression on his face.

"Saturday. Can you pick me up at seven? You'll have to book, though."

Darach gawked at him, obviously surprised that he'd agreed to go out with him, then, having collected himself again, his wonderful smile spread across his features. "You want to come out with me?" he said.

Brice returned his smile. "Yes, if you still want me to."

"Okay, I'm not working, then. I'll ring and hope they can fit us in. It shouldn't be busy at this time of year. I'll be here at seven and we can stow your chair in the back of my SUV. Good — that's good. I'll get off and leave you to it."

"See you Saturday."

Brice watched as Darach backed away then left the workshop. A pool of warmth had settled in his stomach and chest. He smiled then wheeled himself back to the vase and began to plan how he'd turn it into something unique and beautiful.

Chapter Six

Brice opened his wardrobe and stared at its contents.

Princess had immediately taken the opportunity to get into the normally closed space and was sitting staring at him from among the hanging clothes.

"Yes, all right, I know I have a stupid smile on my face. And you like him too, don't deny it. You were rolling around on your back like a complete tart for him."

And instantly he was back to the night before. The memory of their kiss had accompanied him to bed. Half hard already, he'd moved his hand slowly, letting his fingers linger over his skin then, with a vision of Darach McNaughton in his mind, he'd stroked himself to his best climax in—ages.

"Now, what the hell am I going to wear to a posh restaurant?" Princess meowed at him and swished her bushy tail.

"Frankly, you're no help."

She rose and stalked off out of the room.

He didn't own a suit, and jeans wouldn't do. Finally, he remembered a pair of black trousers—the ones he'd worn to court. He could wear them with a black shirt and tie, even if he didn't have a jacket. He found his one pair of shoes and, satisfied with his choices, showered then dressed. He grabbed his black leather coat and waited at the window. A small voice kept trying to worry at the edge of his thoughts, but he pushed it away.

Darach arrived right on time. Brice beat him to the door, wheeled himself out then locked up behind him before rolling down the ramp.

His heart skipped a beat when Darach stepped out of the car. Suited and booted, he appeared like something out of a magazine.

"You scrub up well," Brice said. "I'm sorry, I don't own a suit."

"Why worry? You'd look good in whatever you wore. D'you want me to help you get into the car?"

Brice glanced at the height of the seat. He'd be able to grab the handle above the door and move himself over without too much trouble. "I should be all right, but if you can hold the chair just in case. There are clips on either side, which let you fold it once I'm in the car."

Brice maneuvered himself carefully until he was securely in the passenger seat, leaving Darach to deal with his chair.

"Yep, I can see them," Darach said, clicking the brakes. "I'll stow it in the boot, all right?" He hesitated, and Brice wondered what was coming next.

"If I say anything wrong, please tell me. I don't want to insult you. I know you live by yourself so you can manage, but I don't know you well enough yet, so if I put my foot in it, tell me."

Brice smiled. "Thank you. I can be touchy, I know. I hate having to ask for help, but sometimes it's necessary and I have to bite my tongue. People want to be kind. At least, I'm usually on my own, so they can't talk over me to whoever I'm with as if I'm not there or stupid."

"I'll try to remember."

There were a few cars in the car park when they arrived. Darach pulled into the disabled parking space, climbed out of the driver's seat and brought the wheelchair to the passenger side. Brice maneuvered himself into the seat and followed Darach into the building. A young woman greeted them in reception.

"Welcome to the Lodge, Mr. McNaughton, Mr. Drummond. Your table is ready when you want to be seated, or you can go in the bar and make your choices there."

Darach turned to Brice. "Shall we go straight to the table? As neither of us is drinking, there doesn't seem much point in going to the bar."

"Fine by me."

"Right then, sirs, if you'll follow me."

Brice studied the large room. A few of the tables were occupied, but as Darach had said, January wasn't a popular month for holidays in Scotland. Catriona, as the name tag indicated, showed them to a table by the window. One chair had already been removed and Brice wheeled himself into the space.

"Can I take your coats?"

Brice removed his coat and handed it over as Darach did the same, revealing his dark gray suit teamed with a pale blue open-necked shirt.

"You scrub up well," Brice said.

Catriona handed them the menus and left them to make their choices. Brice scanned the lists, expecting to find little to choose from. He'd had so many vegetarian lasagnas over the years, and he'd never understood why vegetarian food came in the shape of sausages and bacon.

"At least they have a few different choices here," he said. "I'm going to have the tempura vegetables and the potato kiev. I haven't a clue what it will be, but it sounds interesting."

"I hope you don't mind me eating fish. I love the fish around here."

"No, help yourself. I don't impose my beliefs on other people."

"In that case, I'm going to treat myself and have mussels and the sea bass." He waved to the waiter and made their orders.

"So," Brice said, getting in before Darach could ask him anything. "What made you decide to join the police?"

"I think I spent too much time watching cop shows when I was young. I went to university, but it wasn't for me. I'd secretly longed to join the force, but didn't have the guts to tell my parents. In the end, I applied without telling them—*fait accompli*."

"It must be tough dealing with some cases."

"Yeah, it is."

Brice noticed he didn't elaborate. "Is that why you came back here? You don't have to answer if you don't want to."

"Partly. Despite what they show on TV, we don't get many murders, but there are violence and abuse cases. I'm not sure I'll ever get used to how people can be so cruel to each other. Gangs sell drugs and run prostitute rackets, exploiting young men and women. And believe me, there's nothing glamorous when you have to deal with the drunk tank after Celtic plays and someone is sick all over you—or finding an addict with a needle in his arm."

The waiter interrupted them with the food. "This smells so good," Brice said, sniffing.

Darach lifted a mussel with his fork and put it in his mouth. "Oh my, these are gorgeous and the sauce is to die for." Darach ate a few more as Brice cut into his starter.

"Yours okay?" Darach asked.

"Wonderful, so crispy on the outside with crunchy and soft bits. They've even managed to make cauliflower taste interesting. You said work was partly why you left."

Darach sighed and chewed slowly. Brice gazed at his Adam's apple moving when he swallowed his water.

"I split up with my boyfriend."

"Ah, I see. Had you been together long?"

"Seven years. I was planning on maybe getting married, and he was playing away. I caught him and a young constable, fresh out of training, fucking in our bed. It wasn't the first time, but it was the final straw. He'd cheated on me two years before—claimed it was stress over a nasty case—child murder. He works in the Edinburgh division."

Brice sat up. Shit. He'd need to be careful what he said.

"I know there were others, all equally as young, no doubt, and I couldn't take it anymore. Cheating isn't my style. If I'm with someone, I'm with them and that's it."

"So you came back home. I like your sister, and her food."

"Maggie's great—the most level-headed person I know. She's endlessly patient and works so hard. She takes after our mum. My older brother lives in New Zealand now with his wife. They have a huge sheep farm. Maggie and Rob run my dad's farm, cattle and pigs mostly. My mum was a vet. She's retired now. They're great parents. I couldn't have asked for better. I'm worried about Mum, though."

"Is she ill?" Brice thought of his own mother. He had no idea if she was alive or dead. Even when he'd been in the hospital, she'd turned up pissed to visit him and asked if he had any money. He had no idea who his father was and neither did she. It could have been any of the johns she'd turned tricks for. She'd been sixteen when he was born and was already hooked on whatever anyone offered her. She'd tried to clean up her act while she was pregnant, but it hadn't lasted.

Darach pushed his plate away and washed his fingers in the bowl provided. "I think she has the early onset of dementia. I want her to get tested, but she's being stubborn."

"It must be tough for her to face. No one wants to know they've got dementia. I can understand her not wanting to be tested. I've spent enough time around the medical profession." *Fuck! Why did I say that?*

"You didn't mention anything about your parents. Were they in the accident with you?"

Thankfully, the waiter arrived with their main courses. Brice swallowed some water and gazed at the plate of food in front of him. He lifted his fork and tasted.

"This is good," he said, hoping to change the subject. Darach stared at him for a moment before agreeing with Brice as far as the standard of food was concerned. He'd obviously taken the hint. For a while, Brice questioned him about coming out and how his parents had reacted, and they stayed on topics both could deal with—fanciable men, Brice's art, painters who had influenced him. It was good to talk to someone for a change—to explain why he liked

Monet but couldn't stand Dali, and to talk about sculpture and design.

"You're surprisingly knowledgeable for a policeman," Brice said, laughing.

"We're not all Neanderthals. I like art and all types of music, and Glasgow has lots of great places to visit. I've been to Rome, Greece and to the pyramids. History was one subject I did like. Maybe if I'd studied it at university, I'd have stayed, but there aren't many jobs in history unless you want to teach."

"Or work in a museum," Brice said.

"Police work pays better."

They declined desserts and ordered coffee in the bar. The owner came in and introduced himself briefly. Darach seemed a little overwhelmed to meet him and, from a purely esthetic point of view, Brice could see the attraction.

"McKenzie was a great center forward in his day, but gave up because the press was going to oust him. It was all over the news last year. You must have seen it."

"I don't watch much TV," Brice said.

"His ex-boyfriend manages Midchester United—Jed Harris. He came out and their past together became headline news? Harris married his partner here last summer."

"Nope, means nothing to me. He's handsome, though, and he has a great arse."

They both stared at him walking back into the restaurant.

Darach smirked. "You're right. He does."

Brice let Darach pay, as he'd insisted he'd asked him out. On the short journey home, Brice pondered what to do. He liked Darach, but he wasn't ready to share everything with him—not yet. So why, when they arrived back, did he ask him if he wanted to come in?

* * * *

Darach gazed around the living room. The kitchen wall had been removed to create a long room with kitchen blending into dining area then via a narrower archway to the living room, providing light from windows at the front and back. He sat at one end of a sofa designed to make it easier for a person in a chair to get on and off.

"I wasn't sure if you'd have a TV," he said.

Brice came in with a tray attached to the arms of his chair carrying two mugs of coffee. "I bought it to play games on, and I do watch sometimes. I spend most of my time in the workshop with my music for company."

"Ah, a games player. I've never been into computer games. So many seem to be too interested in killing things for my taste. I witnessed enough violence back in Glasgow."

Brice put the coffee down on the table, pulled down the arm of the sofa and moved himself across from his chair. Princess appeared from the bedroom and jumped up to curl in the space between them, allowing her head to loll onto Darach's thigh.

Brice stared at her. "She is a complete tart," he said, rubbing her ears and accidentally making contact with Darach's leg.

"Did you have to have a lot of work done to make this place suitable for you?" Darach asked.

"Some. I had the rooms enlarged and the kitchen and bathroom had to be wheelchair friendly, as did the doorways and the exits. It means I can manage by myself."

"Must have been expensive." Darach was digging and they both knew it.

"The insurance pay-out after the accident covered t." Darach couldn't help noticing Brice didn't meet his gaze when he spoke. As a man trained to interview suspects, he had a feel for when people were lying to him, or not exactly telling the truth. More and more, he suspected Brice was being somewhat economical with the information he provided, and the feeling should bother him more than it did.

"Did you create all these paintings?" he asked, changing the subject.

"Yes, the landscapes around here are beautiful. I especially love the sea when it's stormy, and the sunsets. I drive around with my camera and take photos, or sometimes I'll take out my sketch pad. I painted that one after I was lucky enough to see a group of dolphins at Cullen. I loved watching them leap from the water for the sheer joy of it as the sun was going down behind them—just beautiful. I hope to see them again."

Darach couldn't help himself. He leaned over and put his hand on Brice's cheek, turning his face and kissing him gently. Princess meowed in protest at being squashed and jumped off, letting Darach close the space. He moaned when Brice opened his mouth, allowing Darach to stretch out his tongue and explore. His cock sprang to life, hardening and lessening the space in his trousers. He shifted nearer, letting his hand slip down and land on Brice's thigh. Brushing against Brice's groin, he felt a bulge, which answered one question. Guilt rushed through him and he pulled away. Being with Brice wasn't only about getting his end away, was it?

Before he could say anything, Brice had moved forward and kissed him. This time, both met open-mouthed. Darach could taste coffee on Brice's tongue as he used it to explore Darach's mouth. Brice wrapped his hand around the back of Darach's head, pulling him closer. Unable to stop himself, Darach sucked on Brice's plump, enticing bottom lip, nipping it with his teeth until Brice whimpered. He had no idea how much pain Brice had, or whether he had any feeling in his legs. Conscious of their difference in size, Darach didn't press forward over him just in case he unnerved him. Instead, he reached around and touched Brice's back. His reaction was instantaneous. Brice pulled away to the farthest end of the small sofa, his expression full of fear. Darach had seen the same expression on other faces—on the faces of victims—the abused men, women and children he'd dealt with over the years. *Shit! What did I do?*

"I'm sorry. I thought you wanted... I didn't mean..."

Those blue eyes stared at him. "I want you to go. I can't do this."

Darach noted the shaking hands. He wanted to reach out and tell Brice it was all right—that he understood—but he didn't.

"You can talk to me," he said, his voice a whisper.

"No. I want you to go. I'm no use to you. I'm a cripple in a wheelchair. I'm no use to you. Don't you understand? I can't... I can't give you what you want."

Darach knew this was a lie. He'd felt Brice's erection, but he didn't challenge him.

"All right. I'll go, but don't think I'm just going to abandon you. I don't simply leave friends, and if there's nothing else between us, then I'll settle for friendship, if it's what you want. I guess there are reasons why you chose to come here. I'm not stupid, and I'm sure you'll tell me in your own good time."

"Just go, please." Brice had wrapped his arms around himself and a single tear ran down one cheek. Darach wanted to hug him so much, to take him into his arms, carry him to bed, lay him down, wrap himself around him and scare every single one of his demons away, whatever they were. Him and his superhero complex, as Mitch used to call it.

"I'm going. I'll let myself out. I enjoyed our meal. I like you, Brice, and I'm prepared to wait."

* * * *

Driving home, he decided there had to be a way of finding out more. As soon as he sat on his sofa, he switched on his laptop. Brice had arrived around two years ago, according to Maggie. Maybe there would be some mention of the crash in news archives. He put the name Brice Drummond and car accident into Google, but found nothing. The only thing he knew for certain was that Brice had spent time in

Edinburgh and had moved around Scotland as well. He decided to check the birth records for a Brice Drummond, but found nothing remotely likely, even with different spellings. He put his laptop on the table. Why would Brice be using a false name? Had he been in a crash at all? He was definitely hiding from something or someone.

It was when I went to touch his back. That's when he pulled away. Maybe the crash, if there was one, disfigured him as well as damaging his legs. But why change his name? People usually altered their identities when a crime had happened. Maybe he could get a photograph and show it to Mitch. If Brice had been involved in a crime in Edinburgh, Mitch would know. No, he didn't want to go there — not unless he had to. Darach switched off the computer and trudged upstairs to his bedroom to undress. He stood under the shower, letting the water run down his body, but he still felt cold. Some time passed before the need to sleep overwhelmed him.

Chapter Seven

"What's up? I haven't seen you and Gus for a couple of days. Mel is beginning to think she's done something wrong."

Darach pushed aside the notes he'd been typing up and deliberated upon how to answer his sister. It had been nearly a week since his dinner with Brice had gone pear-shaped.

"We've been busy. The inspector decided we should be more proactive than reactive, so we've been paying visits to known dealers in the area. I'm writing up the notes now. Anyway, Gus tells me that he and Mel are going out tomorrow for a drink, so what's the real reason you've called? I'm sure you're not missing me."

"It's Mum. She didn't want me to tell you or Dad, but yesterday she forgot where she'd left her car. Tosh found her wandering up the high street, trying to find it. She'd parked in front of the supermarket then walked to the card shop. Tosh drove her home. I'm worried, Darach. She needs to see a doctor. I'm thinking of phoning Ellis McKenzie and getting him to come out and have a talk with her. She could have an accident driving, or anything."

Darach sighed. He knew Maggie was right. Even in the few weeks since he'd come back home, he'd witnessed his mother's forgetfulness and instances of confusion.

"I'll invite myself around there tonight. Can you meet me at theirs, or do you want to invite them around for dinner at the farmhouse?"

"So you think there's something wrong too?"

"Yes, Maggie. Remember, I haven't seen her every day

like you have, but I noticed a big difference when I returned. Perhaps we can persuade her to at least talk to Ellis."

"She won't want to give up her car."

"She may have to. I couldn't let her go on driving. She might hurt herself or someone else. Bloody hell, this is so hard. Have you talked to Dad?"

"I tried, but he says he forgets things too, but not like Mum. She's been as sharp as a pin all my life, but she forgot Bobby's name yesterday. Not simply called him everyone's name, but couldn't remember at all until Bobby told her."

"Okay, I'll see you tonight."

"You might want to give Tosh a ring as well—to thank him. He sounded kind of annoyed that you haven't been round there since you returned. I suppose it's a bit awkward with him being married now."

"It's fine," he lied. "I'll ring him when I finish up here. Try not to worry, Mags."

"Yeah, yeah. We'll see you at six. We're having fish and chips."

He put his phone away and stared at the screen. Gus plonked a coffee and paper bag in front of him then leaned on the edge of the desk. Darach sniffed the air hungrily.

"Thought you might want one of these as you've been up all night. I bought us a bacon roll each too."

"You are a lifesaver," Darach replied, ripping open the bag and taking a chunk out of the roll. The grease practically dripped down his throat and he moaned with pleasure. He chewed, slowly savoring the taste. "And this is the reason I could never be a vegetarian," he said. "I like my meat too much."

Gus snickered. "So I've heard."

He and Gus hadn't specifically discussed his sexuality. He usually didn't start every conversation with someone new with the words, 'Hi, I'm Darach and I'm gay.'

"Mel told me—about you being gay. It's all right. I'm fine with it. After all, my best friend is gay. I don't think you're gonna be lusting after my arse any time soon, although it is a rather fine example, if I say so myself. You wouldn't be the first man to admire its shape. Sadly, for them, I'm strictly straight."

"So there's no one you'd bend over for, then — no secret crush." The flush on Gus' cheeks told him he'd hit home. Darach bit off another chunk of bacon roll. Gus recovered quickly and leaned forward. "Well, maybe Tony Stark, you know, Iron Man, especially if Pepper Potts was there as well."

"See?" Darach said. "Everyone has their one."

"Do you have one — a woman, I mean?"

Darach chewed the last bite of bacon roll slowly, as if considering his answer. "Maybe I'll tell you sometime, but now I need to finish this and sleep. Some of us are old and require more rest, you know."

Gus laughed. "You're only, what, five years older than me? Maggie said it's your birthday next month. Will you be having a party for your thirtieth?"

He'd been planning an occasion in Glasgow with Mitch and their friends, but that was off now. "I don't know, Gus. But if I am, you'll get an invite, don't worry."

* * * *

After catching up on his sleep, Darach arrived at the farmhouse dead on six. He wanted to speak to Maggie before his parents arrived, but as soon as he strolled through the door, he realized they'd already arrived and were sat in the main room.

"There he is," his mother said. "Look at you. You've dark circles under your eyes again. I thought you'd come up here to improve your health."

"Sorry, Mum. We've been up all night chasing drug dealers," he said.

"Did you catch any, son?" His father was sitting in his usual armchair. Even though they now lived in the bungalow, the chair was seldom used by anyone other than his father.

"A few small fry, as usual." He lifted his face and sniffed. "Something smells good. I'll go and say hi to Maggie."

His sister stood next to the range. "Rob's out checking on a sow due to farrow at any moment. Hopefully, he'll make it back in time. Dinner will be five minutes. Take the cutlery out, will you, and set the table."

"Where's Bobby?" he asked.

"At Xander's. Those two are joined at the hip, exactly like you and Tosh always were."

Maggie's pensive expression worried him. "It's not genetic, you know – being gay."

"I know. Ignore me, I'm being stupid. This thing with Mum has me all riled up. I wouldn't even care if Bobby was gay, as long as he was happy."

"No one can guarantee happiness, Mags – gay, straight or anything in between." Unbidden, Brice's face jumped into his mind. "Have you seen anything of Brice this week?"

"No, but Princess has been around. I guess your date didn't go well. I didn't like to ask."

"It's complicated," Darach replied. "But I'm not going to give up."

She handed him a bowl of mushy peas. "Here, take this and get the table set up. I'll bring the rest."

They ate the fish and chatted about the farm. Rob appeared with the dogs after ten minutes and joined them so the discussion turned to pigs and the coming lambing season. Darach simply listened, watching his mother and how much she engaged with the conversation, noticing any time she forgot a word or became muddled. He caught a glance from his father and knew he'd seen the same thing. The conversation after dinner wasn't going to be an easy one for any of them.

After a homemade apple pie, they sat together in the main room around the open fire, drinking tea.

"Mum, I want to talk with you about what happened yesterday in town."

His mother stiffened immediately. "It was nothing. I forgot where I'd left the car, that's all."

Darach reached over and grasped her hand. "Mum, you can't go on like this. You're forgetting things."

"Everyone mislays things when they get older. Your father does as well."

"Mum, it's worse than simply losing stuff. You forgot Bobby's name yesterday, and you got agitated when you couldn't find where you'd left something—Dad told me. He says sometimes you don't want to get out of bed, or do anything, and it's not like you, Mum. We're all worried, especially about you driving. We'd like you to make an appointment to see Ellis, or he could come over here, I'm sure. There are tests for—"

"I know what you're saying. You think I've got dementia or Alzheimer's, don't you?"

Darach had hardly ever seen his mother cry. Now tears fell down her cheeks and she clutched his hand tighter. "I know you're scared, Mum, but you can't dig your head in the sand. You're not that sort of person. You've always met everything head on. You're the strongest, most capable person I know." He gazed around the room. His sister wiped away a tear and he wasn't far off crying himself, but they had to face this and deal with it.

"Please, Mum, see Ellis and see what he says. He'll run a few tests."

"All right, all right. I'll ring him on Monday."

"I'll make sure she does," his father added. "And I'm coming too, Peggy. If I'm going to help you, I'll have to know what Ellis says."

Her grip on Darach's hand loosened and she nodded.

"I don't know about anyone else," Darach said. "But my tea's gone cold. Time for a fresh pot."

"I'll make one now," Maggie said. "You can never have too much tea."

"And perhaps a wee dram in it, eh, Stuart?" Rob said, reaching over to the nearby cabinet and taking out a bottle of whiskey.

"Aye, laddie, a little drop wouldn't do any harm before we face the cold outside."

* * * *

Later, after his parents had returned to their bungalow, he sat with Maggie and Rob next to the fire. The dogs snored away, basking in the heat on the rug.

"At least she has agreed to go," he said. "I wasn't sure whether we were going to have to stage an intervention and get Ellis here in secret."

"I think she was more shaken up by the event yesterday than she's admitting. It must be so scary to forget where you are, especially when you know you should remember. That's the worst part of something like this — knowing your mind is going and not being able to do a damn thing about it. It's so bloody unfair." Rob put his arm around Maggie.

"We'll do all we can, love. And at least she's not on her own, and she has her family around. She's so glad you've come home, Darach. She missed you, and now Gray is away as well…"

Darach stood. "It's been a long day, Mags. I'll call you to see how she is. I'm going to give Tosh a ring when I get home, so I'd better get off as I'm on early tomorrow."

Maggie accompanied him to the door. He hugged her and opened it. The freezing air hit him immediately. "It's still cold enough for snow," he said.

"I hope not. We lose lambs if it snows and we haven't managed to reach the ewes in time, even though we've brought them close to the farm now."

"If Brice comes into the café, would you give me a ring?" he asked, trying to keep his tone casual.

"Sure. Planning to surprise him?"

"Something along those lines," he said. He had a plan. Maybe he shouldn't, but his curiosity compelled him to try to find out Brice's true identity for his own peace of mind.

He waved from the car, shifted it into gear, and set off home in the dark.

Chapter Eight

Tosh and Harry lived over the shop. Darach parked his car at the front and glanced down the road to where Brice lived, relieved to see light in the front window. That morning, Maggie had called him to let him know Brice had turned up at the café and purchased his usual supplies. Luckily, he and Gus hadn't been far away, and although he'd have died from embarrassment if anyone had seen him hiding behind a tree with a long lens, he'd managed to take a few shots with enough detail for Brice to be recognized.

"Should I ask?" Gus had questioned.

"I'd rather you didn't."

"I'll assume there's nothing criminal I should be aware of."

"No, there isn't. At least I don't think there is."

"Because this could be breaking the law. It's certainly an invasion of privacy."

Darach had turned to the constable. "I have my reasons, Gus. I need you to turn a blind eye to this one. I don't intend to do anything bad with the photographs."

"Okay, but this is the only time. I don't know how you do things in Glasgow, but we don't do this without good reason around here."

"Your concern is noted, and if there's anything you should know, I'll fill you in as much as necessary."

Later, he'd emailed the photographs to Mitch. He figured his ex owed him, and he didn't want to go through official channels. Brice had mentioned Edinburgh, giving him the only lead he had. He told himself he was acting to protect Brice, whatever the circumstances. If he was in trouble,

Darach wanted to help. He didn't want whatever it was to come between them. That's what he told himself.

Tosh opened the door to him seconds after he'd pressed the buzzer. When he'd called and suggested that they meet up, he'd been relieved to find out Harry wouldn't be there, because he was on a buying trip at a big fair down in Dumfries the day after. He followed Tosh up the stairs.

"Stop ogling my arse," Tosh said without any ire in his voice.

"Then stop wiggling it in my face," Darach replied, laughing. They'd been friends since their mothers had given birth in the same ward hours apart. Their relationship had only changed when they were sixteen.

"Here we are," Tosh said, showing him into the main room. "It's not huge, but it's home."

Darach gazed around the room with its colorful décor and leather sofas. One wall was filled with books, and another with a huge collection of single flower vases.

"Harry's a collector, I see."

"We both are. My Marvel comic characters are in the bedroom. Antiques of the future, Harry calls them. I've made us lasagna. I remember how much you liked Italian."

"Still do, and you always liked cooking. I thought you might become a chef."

"I considered it, but the hours are mad, and there aren't a lot of opportunities around here. I didn't want to leave. I enjoy being a postman most of the time. I'm still an early riser." Tosh smirked before turning back to the cooker.

Memories of early-morning sex flooded into Darach's mind. He grinned. "I remember."

"Luckily for me, Harry is a morning person as well." The wink told Darach all he needed to know.

"Sit. I'll get us a drink."

Darach noted Tosh had brought both of them fizzy water. "I'm sorry I didn't come to the wedding. I was going through some stuff with Mitch, and I wasn't ready to deal with you and Harry being all lovey-dovey with each other, when I'd just split up with my boyfriend."

"Must have been tough." Tosh sat on the other sofa.

"It wasn't the first time he'd been unfaithful, but this time he'd brought the twink home and fucked him in our bed. It was too much, and I knew he wanted out. This was his way of telling me we were over."

"Extreme, but obviously effective. I have the wedding photos if you want to see them."

"Why not. I could do with seeing happy people for a change." He explained they'd spoken to his mother about what had happened.

"It's good she's going to see Doctor McKenzie. I was glad I could help her out. I've always admired your mum. She and your dad didn't bat an eyelid when they found out you and I were boyfriends, and your mum talked to my parents. She helped me."

Tosh came and sat next to him with a large book. "We had an album made rather than only having something digital."

Darach opened the book and smiled. "You wore the Mackintosh tartan, then?"

"I did. And no crack about me wearing the dress. Harry refused to show his knees in public so went for the suit instead."

"I wouldn't dream of assuming your sexual preferences from you wearing a kilt. As I recall, you were rather versatile." He turned the pages, examining each picture containing Tosh's family and their friends. As Tosh had stayed local, unlike Darach, he'd kept in contact with all their friends. Darach scrutinized face after face discussing whether they'd changed, kept their hair, put on weight, or stayed exactly the same. "From the smile on your faces in every photo, I'd say you had a good day."

"We did. The Lodge does great weddings. But you know about the food yourself. I understand you were there with Brice the other night. Small place — people talk, and I am the local postman. So — you and him?"

"I don't know. We had a great dinner, and I thought...

Then he told me to leave."

"What did you do?"

"Nothing. We kissed a few times. It was good. Then he told me he couldn't, and implied he wasn't able to — you know."

"Perform?"

"Yeah, but I know he was lying. There was a definite hard-on in his trousers. And there's something else. I wanted to find out about his accident. I tried to see if I could find any information online, but there was nothing with his name, so I checked the birth records and he doesn't exist." A familiar expression crossed his friend's face. One that questioned his actions and feared for his safety. Darach leaned forward. "This is between you and me, all right? I know you're thinking I should walk away and not get involved. I can tell from your face."

"Since when did you ever listen to me? You always did what you wanted to do in the end, whatever I thought." It wasn't hard for Darach to hear the resentment in those words. "He must have reasons for keeping quiet."

A buzzer sounded in the kitchen and Tosh rose. "Give me a few minutes."

Darach sat wondering how much he should tell Tosh. Despite the comments, he trusted him implicitly. Tosh returned with bowls of lasagna and a plate of dough balls on a large tray.

"This smells good," Darach said. He ate for a few minutes, dipping the dough balls into the cheese and tomato sauces, waiting for Tosh to say something.

"I get the feeling there's something you want to ask me, Dar. Cards on the table. You know I can't tell you who he gets post from unless this is official police business, and it isn't, is it?"

"No, and I don't want to ask around at work for obvious reasons. I know you can't tell me anything, but you've talked to him. Has he said anything to you about his past?"

"All I know is he ended up in the chair because of an

accident soon after passing his driving test."

"He told me the same story."

"Then maybe that's what happened. Maybe he changed his name because he didn't like the original one. It's not illegal, you know."

"But why would he move here? He's, what, early twenties? And he brings himself to the backend of nowhere. He told me his family moved around, but he's originally from Edinburgh. He's been deliberately vague about everything. Maybe it's the cop in me, but I can't leave things. I know he likes me so why did he push me away? What if something happened to him? My mind is all over the place imagining. He could have been assaulted, or abused, or anything, and by my actions, I've made it worse. I want to help him, Tosh."

"He won't appreciate you taking pity on him because of the chair. One thing I do know is that he's totally independent. He's also got talent. Tourists buy each piece he makes, and they often ask if he has a website."

"And there's another weird thing. You'd think he'd have a website to sell his work, but he doesn't. He could sell his stuff anywhere, all over the country. He did this portrait of me after meeting me a couple of times, and it's stunning."

"You have this bad, don't you? Never lost your habit of falling fast, going from zero to a hundred in seconds. Look at what happened with us. I'd fancied you for ages and nothing. I didn't even know you were gay. Then one night you put your arm around me and bingo—everything changed. It wasn't as if it was the first time we'd touched or anything."

"I know, but I had no idea you were gay either. We'd kept secrets from each other. I put my arm around you and it was as if a light switched on in my brain. I thought about nothing but you all the next day."

"Then you kissed me the day after and I dropped to my knees, not wanting to let a chance go by in case you changed your mind."

"We learned a lot together, didn't we, you and I? Do

you think we'd have stayed together if I hadn't gone to university?"

Tosh shrugged. "I don't know, but it doesn't matter now."

Darach reached over and put his hand on Tosh's arm. "I'm glad you found someone. You deserve to be happy, even if you have married someone with no arse."

"He has enough for my requirements, and he makes up for his lack of arse elsewhere."

"Does he, indeed?" Darach said, laughing.

Tosh smiled and gazed off into the distance. "Oh, yeah."

They both laughed.

"Good for you," Darach said, grinning from ear to ear.

"Oh, he is," Tosh replied, returning his grin.

They reminisced about old times, their families, local sports teams, what had happened to their school friends, who had married whom, and who was divorced. By ten-thirty, Darach realized he'd laughed more than he had for ages.

"It's been good catching up," he said. "I'd better get off. I'm painting my bedroom tomorrow."

"Need any help? I'm a dab hand with a paintbrush."

"I'd love some. Two will get it done quicker than one. I'll even provide food," Darach said.

* * * *

Back home, he checked his emails. Mitch's name jumped off the screen. He opened up the message.

I have information but I need to see you. Can you get to Glasgow ASAP?

Darach had a couple of days off the week after on Tuesday and Wednesday. He fired off a reply agreeing to meet Mitch at their local pub. He ran his fingers through his hair. What the hell could it be that Mitch had to tell him in person? And how was he going to survive until Tuesday night to find out?

Chapter Nine

Darach found a booth at the back of the pub. He didn't want anyone overhearing the conversation. With his mother's visit to the doctor and his worrying about what Mitch would say to him, it had been a long couple of days. He nursed his bottle of Coke and ate cheese and onion crisps. He'd been around to his parents' last night. His mother had gone to bed early.

"Give her time, Darach. This is hard for her. Ellis wants her to go for more tests, and you know how much she hates the medical profession and people poking and prodding at her. She has to get her head around this and work out a plan. You know what she's like."

He'd nodded and shared a drink with his father, knowing he too was going to have to face up to the possibility of losing his wife mentally, if not physically. Dementia had many forms. He glanced up when a shadow loomed over his table. It had only been a matter of weeks since he'd seen Mitch but he appeared thinner. Every few minutes, he'd glance around, a worried expression on his face.

"D'you want another one of them?" Mitch asked. From the half-empty pint glass he held, he'd obviously made a start himself.

"I'd rather have something to eat. I seem to remember they do battered chicken curry pie here—heart attack on a plate. I'll have one of them and chips with peas to keep up my fiber intake. I'd say you could use a square meal. You've lost weight." He shouldn't care, but for him, Mitch looked better carrying a few extra pounds.

"I'll go get us something, then." Mitch put his glass on the table and turned around.

Minutes later, he returned and settled down, putting a tumbler of whiskey next to his pint. "You're looking good, Dar. The move has gone well, then?"

"It's good to be back with my family, but I do miss the bright lights. Would you mind if we cut the small talk and get to why we're here? I want to know what you know about him, and why I had to come down here to find out."

A waitress brought their food to the table. Darach ate a few chunks of the pie and chips, waiting for Mitch to speak. The man appeared worried and kept glancing around, as if he expected someone else to be there. In the end, he couldn't wait any longer.

"You seem nervous, Mitch. What the hell is going on?"

"The guy in the photograph. I'm surprised you don't remember yourself, although I suppose they did keep the details out of the press. He was a witness in the case against the gang leader Tommy Mahon. I don't know all the details of the case, but his evidence resulted in Mahon being sent down for fifteen years."

"Has he always been in the chair?"

"No, someone leaked his name and some of Mahon's gang beat him up to stop him from giving evidence. The case was delayed until he recovered. For a while, it was touch and go, but his overall health improved and he received protection. He had a handler to look after him for a while, but I doubt she'll tell you anything. He's still being protected as the people who beat him up are still at large. No doubt someone at your station will be his liaison now that so much time has passed since the actual case."

Darach chewed his food, mulling over everything he'd heard so far. "So he risked his life to help put away a bastard who sold drugs to kids and ran prostitute rings with underage boys and girls. Was...?" He stopped, not wanting to use Brice's new name. "What was his name?"

"Jimmy Boyden. I've no idea what his name is now, and don't tell me."

"Have you told me everything?"

Mitch glanced around again. "There were reasons why he gave evidence against Tommy."

"What? Other than the fact that the man was a complete monster?"

"You know the murder of the six-year-old girl, Stacey MacDonald? We caught the bastard by accident after a traffic cop stopped him. Stacey wasn't his first victim. He confessed to the murder of Sadie Boyden. She was the eight-year-old sister of Jimmy Boyden. He was sixteen when his sister was killed. His mother had been one of Tommy's girls for years – working to maintain her habit and to pay for the alcohol. I worked the case. We had a tip-off, it turns out from Tommy Mahon, but he lied to us for reasons of his own. I don't know all the details."

"So Jimmy gave evidence because Tommy had let the man who murdered his sister go free. Sounds like a bloody complicated web of deception. No wonder he wanted to get away from there. Thanks. This information explains some things." *But not others.* After ten minutes, Mitch had hardly touched his food, simply pushing it around his plate.

"How are you doing, Mitch?"

"I've sold the flat – couldn't manage the mortgage after all, not on my own. I'm renting a two-bedroom flat not far from here. Work's nonstop. The new inspector is a stickler for the rules – wants every 'i' dotted and every 't' crossed." He stopped and stared at Darach. "I miss you. We were good together."

"But not good enough for you to keep your dick out of some twink's willing arse. He'd only been in the force a matter of weeks. Probably thought he was advancing his career. He was eighteen and green as grass and you couldn't resist plowing virgin territory, could you? And I know it wasn't the first time. After we split, a few of your colleagues helpfully filled me in with other examples from when you worked vice. Putting your own health in danger was one thing, but mine as well? I'm glad we used condoms after all, because you said you preferred it. I should have known you were putting it about elsewhere. What man prefers latex? I refused to see what was staring me in the face. Your loss, though."

"I suppose you have a right to be angry."

Darach clutched his thigh, digging his fingers in to stop himself from shouting. They'd done enough shouting. He clenched his teeth and lowered his voice. "Talk about a bloody understatement."

"You screwing Jimmy, then? Rumor was he wasn't fussy about who fucked his pretty arse. I suppose it doesn't matter if he's only half a man."

Darach formed his hands into fists. He wanted to do nothing more than punch the smirk from his ex-boyfriend's face. Instead, he moved to the end of the booth. "Don't forget to pay on the way out. I appreciate the information. Have a good life, Mitch. I hope you find the happiness you're searching for. I guess you can use some. I don't expect we'll see each other again." He rose then strode across the bar and didn't glance back. He had answers, but he knew there was more. Somehow he had to get Brice to talk if they were to have any sort of relationship, and he wanted something from the man. Maybe he had something to offer him too.

* * * *

"I'm having the nightmares again." Brice sat in a large wing-backed armchair. Outside, the rain made the already bleak granite buildings of Aberdeen seem grayer still. It had been months since he'd seen Alisha, but he needed to talk to someone and it was her or his police handler, so coming here had seemed preferable.

"Has something happened to start them up again?" the psychologist asked. "Do you feel you're in danger? Has someone tried to contact you from your old life, because you need to let your liaison know if you're worried?"

"No, it's nothing like that." He hesitated. Alisha appeared

like everyone's mother with her hair swept up in a bun held together with what looked like chopsticks. This innocent image belied her raunchier nature with her easy use of vulgar language and descriptions of even the mostly seemingly extreme sexual acts. For him, she'd been a rock. She had never judged him and he'd given her plenty to judge. She'd listened to what had happened and to what he'd done.

"So what is it, then?" she asked, leaning forward from her own chair.

"I've met someone. We kissed, he touched me, and I froze and threw him out. I can't reveal details of the case, or what happened to me, or what I did — and he's a cop."

"Ah. But you have a contact in the local police, don't you? Maybe you should let them know, then he can know, and it might not be a problem."

"I doubt they'd be pleased to have one of their own getting involved with me, for obvious reasons, but it's more than simply revealing who I am. I can't explain away everything by telling him about the beating. The choices I made after Sadie died. I have to live with those choices."

"You were young, Brice. You blamed yourself for something you had no control over."

"But if I'd been there. If I'd stopped Mum from drinking and getting high. If I'd kept her away from Tommy Mahon. If I'd met Sadie from school. If she hadn't been on her own and snatched off the street that bastard wouldn't have been able to..." His body shook as tears flowed down his face and he wrapped his arms around his frame.

"Brice, you know you weren't responsible for Sadie's death, or what that monster did to her or the other girl."

"But he told me he'd sorted it. Tommy told me he'd put him down, then I found out he'd lied to me. I'd let him do all those things he did to me for four years because I thought I owed him...and to punish myself."

She stared at him, knowing he was being economical with the truth of the relationship between him and Tommy.

Complicated didn't even scratch the surface.

"But at least they're both behind bars now, Brice, and you helped put them there, both Sadie's murderer and Tommy Mahon. The other girl's death wasn't your fault. You did your best. Your bravery, even after the beating, even after they tried to stop you giving evidence against Tommy, helped to put them both away."

"I keep seeing them, Dean and his cronies, standing around me, kicking me and spitting and pissing on me, and they're still out there. I can't go back home. I've lived for two years in the back of beyond, not letting anyone near me for fear of being discovered. I'm stuck in this chair because of them, but there wasn't enough evidence to put them behind bars—they all had alibis. Tommy may have been a sadist, but Dean is one sick, twisted bastard. He hated me, called me names, didn't seem to understand if I was a faggot then so was his uncle Tommy, who was fucking me day and night. I might have had long blond hair, but everyone knew I was Tommy's boy."

"You did what you thought you had to do. Maybe it's time to let someone into your life and tell him who you were. You told me you're not ashamed of being gay."

"I'm not."

"Are you sure?"

Brice shifted in the chair. Was he sure? Being gay had never brought him anything good in his life, after all. He swallowed hard. "Being gay is who I am. I can't change and I don't want to. No one is going to make me ashamed of my sexuality."

"Good. That's the Brice I know. What Dean did to you wasn't because you're gay, not really, it was just another stick to beat you with. He simply wanted power over you, that's all. To show you he was stronger than you, and to punish you for the influence you'd had over his uncle. What are you going to do?"

"I'll talk to the inspector, but I have to talk to Darach as well. We've no future unless I tell him the truth, and if he can't live with it, then we didn't have a future anyway."

Alisha fixed him with another of her challenging stares. "Go easy on him, Brice. You know what you were like when you first came to see me, how you tried to shock me with how you dressed and what you revealed."

Brice laughed. "And you never batted an eyelid, despite everything, and all my acting out."

"Learn to give yourself a pat on the back occasionally." She glanced over to the brightly colored vase sitting on the windowsill. "You're a talented young man, Brice Drummond, with your whole life in front of you. If there's one thing I've learned in this job, it's you can't change the past, but you can influence the future."

"Maybe I'll go shopping and buy myself a new suit," Brice said. He moved himself back into his chair and began to wheel himself out of the room.

"Good idea. You should get out more. Ring me, Brice — I worry about you. Don't leave it so long next time. And remember, go gently."

Chapter Ten

January turned into February then March, and still Darach did nothing. He spent his free time doing up his house, painting it from top to bottom. Twice a day, every day, he drove past Brice's house. Sometimes he stopped at his sister's café, hoping Brice might appear and they could talk on neutral ground. Some nights he'd park his car and watch from a distance, seeing a shadow cross the curtained window, pleased to know Brice was alive.

He was sitting drinking coffee one morning after he'd been on the night shift when the door opened and Princess hopped onto the windowsill. She nudged his elbow with her head and he put cut-up bacon down in front of her.

"I wish you could speak," he said, scratching her ears. "I wish you could tell me how he is and what he's doing." She sat and meowed at him. He'd read somewhere that cats only meowed at humans and not to each other. "Maybe you are trying to tell me something — probably how we're both idiots. Cats know best." Princess curled up and settled herself down to sleep.

"He doesn't come in here much anymore," Maggie said, sitting adjacent to him while Mel manned the counter. "Why don't you go and see him?"

"He told me to go."

"Oh, for goodness sake. Men! You're being a stupid, stubborn git. You like him, don't you?"

"It's not exactly simple, Maggie. There are things I can't tell you about — police things. I know I can trust you but... I just can't."

"Okay. I did wonder when he appeared seemingly out

of nowhere whether he was running away from a bad situation."

"Don't try to wheedle it out of me, Mags. I know what you're like, and a Chinese burn isn't going to work. I'm glad he's all right, that's all, and at least you let me know when he's been in." He yawned. "I'd better get off home and get to bed. They've forecast snow for later, and with this bitter wind, I wouldn't be surprised if we get blizzard conditions."

"I'm going to close up as soon as it begins," Maggie said. "Rob's brought the sheep indoors now. Last thing we want is ewes giving birth out in these conditions."

"March comes in like a lion, don't they say? Winter certainly appears to be having one last hurrah Make sure you do leave for home on time. And if you can, check Princess gets home as well." He stood and waved to Mel.

"Gus is coming to pick Mel up after lunch. She blathers on and on about him."

"He's the same. It's Mel this and Mel that. He's invited me to Sunday lunch with his family."

"What? All of them?"

"Jeez, I hope not." He kissed her cheek. "I'll see you soon, sis."

After a few hours' sleep and something to eat, he glanced out of the window at the falling snow. He shivered, even though the room was warm. After grabbing his coat, he went outside and climbed into his car. He'd bought a four-wheel-drive especially for conditions like these. He drove the quickest way to Brice's house. The café windows were dark. At least his sister had gone before conditions underfoot deteriorated. He drove nearer to the house. The window was dark there too, so maybe Brice was in his workshop. Worried, he decided to go around the back to check. A dark shape appeared on the wall and began to cry pitifully — Princess. What on earth was she doing out there, damp and covered in flakes of snow? Her wailing continued, leaving him no choice. He dragged himself out of the car and she immediately trotted to the back then turned to meow again.

"Okay, okay, I hear you."

There were no lights on in the workshop either. He picked up speed, turning the corner to the back of the house. He gasped at the sight in front of him. Brice lay sprawled on the path, his wheelchair on its side. Darach rushed and pulled Brice's head into his lap, calling his name.

"Get me up," Brice said. "So cold."

Happy that he was conscious, Darach stood and lifted Brice, carrying him into the living room and putting him on the sofa. Princess immediately jumped up beside her owner and began to press against him.

"My chair," Brice said.

Darach rushed outside again, picked up the chair and closed the door behind him. He turned up the heat and hurried back into the room.

"We need to get you out of these wet things and warmed up," he said. "How long have you been out there?" He lifted Brice once more and carried him through to his bedroom and set him down on the bed. He quickly grabbed two large towels from the bathroom and rubbed Brice's hair dry. "Your hands are freezing. Let's get these damp things off you."

"The chair got caught and I couldn't move it. Must have misjudged in the snow."

"You should have an emergency contact. Why didn't you phone the police? They'd have sent someone out to you."

"I couldn't find my phone. It must have fallen out in the snow," Brice replied through chattering teeth.

"Right, let's get you out of these things."

Brice kept his arms at his sides. "It's all right. I can manage. I don't need you here. Thank you for rescuing me, but I don't require a hero."

"I'm not a bloody hero, and you're shivering. You need to get out of these clothes, get into bed, and drink warm tea or soup. Let me help you. Don't be so fucking stubborn."

"Is that how you've been trained to speak to the public,

Sergeant McNaughton?"

"No," Darach replied in a softer tone. "Only people who need it. Now," he said, grabbing the edges of Brice's jumper and T-shirt, "let's get these off."

Brice held up his arms. Darach pulled the clothes over Brice's head, threw them into the corner and stared.

"I assume you're staring at my tattoos and piercings."

"Well, yes, I knew you had some from the one on your neck, but I didn't expect... I'll go and get us mugs of tea. Can you get yourself into bed?"

"I do every night," Brice snapped.

Darach returned to the kitchen, got the tea things ready and leaned against the counter, waiting for the kettle to boil. Practically the whole of Brice's chest and upper arms were covered in tattoos, mostly of flowers, interwoven together. Against his pale skin, they were incredible. Then there were the rings through each nipple. Jesus, his cock had jumped on sight. He took a few deep breaths to try to get himself back together, and made the tea. The mugs warmed his hands as he carried them back to Brice's bedroom.

On entering the room, the gasp flew out of his mouth before he could stop it and liquid sloshed over the sides of the mugs. Brice was sitting, naked, on the edge of the bed, with his back turned to the door. "Oh, my God. Did he do that to you? I expected you'd have marks after the beating, but not this..."

Brice turned to face him, seemingly oblivious to his nakedness, his eyes wide with fear and shock. "You know who I am?"

Darach wanted to move nearer, but he remained rooted to the spot, unsure of what to say. "Yes, I did some digging." He didn't want to tell Brice how he'd found out, to protect him and Mitch. He glanced down at the mugs.

"I made us both tea."

He moved slowly forward, put the mugs on a chest of drawers, and sat on the bed next to Brice, leaning so he could see the crisscrossed pattern of scars on Brice's back.

He wanted to touch them, as if his hand could wipe them all away. "At least the bastard was imprisoned for a long time," he said.

Brice glared at him.

"He's not doing time for those," he said finally, getting into the bed and pulling the covers over himself until only his head showed. Darach couldn't have described the expression on Brice's face if he'd tried—defiance? Was that what Brice was trying to project? His stare unnerved Darach, but he couldn't turn away.

"I begged for those marks—all of them, on my hands and knees, if he wanted me to. I craved each stripe of the whip or cane across my back—every beating, every flogging, every time he wanted me to crawl to him, or take his dick in my mouth. Every time he fucked me, however, wherever, was because I let him, and because I persuaded myself I loved him and deserved the pain he willingly handed out."

"What?" Darach rose from the bed and backed away in horror, not wanting to believe what he'd heard. "No, it's not possible." However, he couldn't stop himself from lifting his head to meet Brice's eyes.

Brice uncovered his chest and arms. "I would have done anything for him. I thought I owed him, so I gave him the only thing I had to give—me. Can't you understand, Sergeant? Wouldn't you want the same? Me, cuffed to the bed, face down, arse in the air, ready for you to fuck me into the mattress, or trussed up like a chicken, or lashed to a cross or bench, unable to move. Wouldn't you want someone who would do whatever you wanted, no matter how perverse? I can see it from the expression on your face and the bulge in your jeans that you would. There it is. The look—revulsion mixed with that little bit of excitement."

"I don't understand." Darach's mind whirled with everything crashing around him. This couldn't be true. It didn't make any sense. "But you shopped him to the police. It was your evidence they used to put him away. I thought—"

"That I did it because of the beating, which left me crippled like this? No, the beating happened after I went to the police."

"I know it did. I thought you gave evidence because of your sister, because Tommy had sent the wrong man to prison. I thought you wanted revenge when the other girl was killed." Darach had no idea what to do. He wanted to get out of there, but his legs refused to move. How had he been so wrong? Why hadn't Mitch filled him in about Brice and Tommy? Did he know? Mitch had worked vice, after all.

He glanced back at Brice. Something had changed — the defiance had dissipated and had been replaced. Tears streamed down Brice's stricken face. "I didn't know there was another girl until after I'd been to the police, until after I'd left him. I didn't know the bastard had told me lies to get me into his bed, to make me grateful, to make me hate myself even more for letting her get killed. For four years I was his, his pet, his whipping boy, taking the pain he handed out — my punishment. Only what I deserved for letting Sadie down, letting that bastard take her and do the things he did to her. Tommy told me he'd sorted it and that he'd make sure my mother was taken care of. He became my whole world. I didn't go out. I had no knowledge of anything unless he wanted me to know. He liked to boast, to tell me things — what he'd done and to whom. I became invisible to him, like a servant in a great house, waiting in the darkness until my presence was demanded. Meanwhile, I stored up every single snippet of information."

"So why did you turn against him if it wasn't because of your sister or how he treated you?" The question was spoken out loud before Darach could stop himself.

Brice stuck out his chin and wiped his bloodshot eyes now circled with red. "I did it because he'd found another boy. He liked them young and pretty, and I'd become too old for him, had too many scars. He wanted a fresh canvas to work with. I gave him up to the coppers because I was jealous. I found out everything else later—how he'd lied to me and used me. His nephew Dean and a few cronies did this. I ended up in the hospital for months. I'm pinned together now, but they kicked my lower spine so badly I couldn't move my legs. I suppose I'm lucky they didn't aim higher. I have more control than many. At least I can still pee and shit when I want, and my dick still functions. But tell me, Sergeant, who would want this body? Would you now that you've seen it all?"

Darach opened his mouth, but found he had no words.

"The police offered me protection after the beating and I ended up here in the arse end of nowhere. Tommy had allowed me certain things to keep me amused as well as the drugs to keep me quiet and placid. Nothing too strong—he wanted me to feel the pain he inflicted. He liked it when I screamed. I learned to make pottery and to paint. I'd spent half my childhood in galleries keeping warm. Now I make money from it—enough to keep me and Princess anyway."

Darach glanced around the room at the paintings adorning the walls. They were mostly landscapes like the ones he'd painted for others, but among them were a few portraits. The young man they depicted was obvious to anyone who cared to see.

"You painted these?" Darach asked.

Brice nodded.

"They're beautiful. You were beautiful." He stopped. "I mean…"

"It's all right, Darach." It was the first time Brice had used his name. "I was beautiful, and now I'm merely the person you see before you. I don't want or need your pity. I made my own choices. I think you should go now. You know the truth about me. Your inspector knows who I am as well. I'll tell him and square everything with him. I'll tell him I told you who I am. I'm sure it won't cause you any problems."

Darach glanced into the corner of the room where a rack of paintings stood next to the wall. "Are there more in here?" he asked, ignoring Brice's instructions.

"There are, but they're for my eyes only. Please. Leave them."

Darach pulled two canvases apart. "Shit!"

"I told you not to look."

"Is this you?" The painting was of a young man bound in an intricate set of ropes and knots, his head hanging down, red marks across his pale skin. The image was as beautiful as it was disturbing.

"So, now you know all the deep, dark, dreadful secrets of the local recluse. Thank you for helping me. If you could make sure the door is closed on your way out, I can manage now."

Darach pulled the curtain and stared out the window. The snow had fallen quickly, with several inches covering the road and his car. He turned back to check on Brice. Without speaking, he crossed the floor and made his way to the other side of the bed. He removed his clothes piece by piece until he stood naked, then pulled back the duvet. He waited for Brice to protest, but he said nothing. Instead, he turned over with his back to Darach. Taking his acquiescence as a signal, Darach climbed into the bed and traced some of the scars with his finger, feeling each ridge and bump until Brice reached around and grabbed his hand, pulled it to his chest and wove their fingers together.

"You can make me breakfast in the morning," Darach whispered into Brice's ear. "I like my bacon extra crispy." He sighed then closed his eyes, unable to keep the lids from falling shut.

Chapter Eleven

Brice moved himself out of Darach's arms and reached for the container. He hoped not to wake the man sleeping behind him. Most of him couldn't get his head around the fact that Darach was there. Getting out of bed and going to the bathroom in the dark was too complicated to contemplate so he relieved himself into the large plastic bottle he kept under the bed. The bed dipped behind him.

"Brice?" a deep voice questioned.

"Stay where you are," Brice said, finishing and putting the lid back on the bottle. "I had to piss. I didn't want to wake you by getting up."

"We should talk," Darach said.

A warm hand touched his back and Brice shivered.

"Do we have to? Didn't I do enough talking last night?" He wasn't sure what to do now. Should he get up anyway? He didn't want to. All he wanted to do was feel those arms around him again.

"Maybe not now," Darach agreed, "but..."

Brice grabbed the handle on the headboard and pulled himself back into the bed to face Darach in the darkness. His eyes had adjusted, allowing him to make out the shape and position of the other man's features.

"Why did you stay? After what I said, all that I told you. You should have run screaming, especially after seeing..."

Darach sighed and Brice held his breath, waiting to hear what he'd say.

"Do you want the truth?" Darach asked.

"I suppose it's only fair after me confessing my darkest secrets." He breathed deeply in an effort to control the rising panic in his chest. "Okay, give me your worst."

"The truth is I don't know. I could say I didn't want to have to go out into the snow, but I suppose I thought you needed someone, and maybe I did too. Don't get me wrong. I don't understand why you allowed him to treat you like a possession. I know people like pain. I know there are people who like dressing in nappies or having their cocks kept in cages. I've always been a 'whatever floats your boat' sort of person, as long as you remain within the law, but there's knowing and there's understanding. I don't understand. You say you loved him. I heard the same from a woman whose husband abused and finally killed her. She wouldn't leave him and it cost her her life."

"I'm not saying it's the same, but there's a freedom in letting someone control you. He fed me, told me I looked pretty, what a good boy I was, how I pleased him. If I did wrong, he punished me."

"But you gave him up because he found someone else, even though you say you loved him?"

Brice longed to reach out and touch Darach, but he kept his hands to himself. "Love and hate – not much difference at times. I thought I'd end up on the streets. I had nothing but my body to sell, and who would want to buy damaged goods like me?"

Darach remained silent for a while then lifted his arm. Brice laid his head on Darach's chest and breathed out slowly. Why, after all he'd been through, was he so scared? He traced his fingers down Darach's chest only to have a hand stop him immediately below the belly button.

"There's no need," Darach said.

"Maybe I want to."

Darach lifted his hand and placed it on Brice's stomach. His cock lurched upward in response as Darach traced circles around his navel then tracked across his hip bones, finally landing on Brice's now-erect cock.

"You don't have to either," Brice said.

"Let me," Darach whispered. "Let me do something nice

for you."

"Why not do something nice for both of us? Hold us together. Bring us both off. I want to feel you next to me. I want to hear you come." It had been so long.

"Shit! I'm so hard now," Darach said while moving closer. He held their cocks with one hand.

"Help me," he said. Brice moved his hand to work with Darach's, stroking up and down, spreading pre-cum from them both to aid movement. He glanced up and his gaze met Darach's. The space closed between them as Darach placed his mouth on Brice's and demanded entry with his tongue. Brice let him explore, opened his mouth wider, tasting mint, then, worrying his morning breath might be overpowering, he pulled away.

"I must taste rank," he managed between breaths. He wasn't used to kissing. Tommy didn't kiss – ever.

"Don't care," Darach replied, taking hold of Brice's bottom lip with his teeth and tugging gently. Sucking turned to nipping and kisses along Brice's jaw line and anywhere else Darach could reach while their hands worked together, until one after the other they came, spirting hot liquid over their hands and stomachs. Brice lay still. Only the sound of breathing filled the room along with the smell of sex. This was different. Brice couldn't have said why in words. He'd had orgasms as intense before, his injuries hadn't taken his ability to feel away from him. Maybe it was having no pain, no residual ache from what had been done to him so he could concentrate everything on the pleasure. It wasn't as if he hadn't wanked himself every now and again in an effort to remind himself that he was still alive.

"Are you all right?" Darach asked. "You've gone quiet on me."

"I'm good. It's only… I haven't… Not with anyone else… in so long."

Darach moved next to him and reached over him to turn on the lamp. "I can't say I'm happy with what you told me last night, and it'll take me time to get my head around everything, but I want to. I'm a good listener. But if you need that…I don't know…lifestyle, I can't offer it to you. It's not in me — well, maybe some, but not all. I'm not naïve enough to think we can start something together and ignore the past. I know we'll have problems to overcome, mentally and physically. I've only recently come out of a disastrous relationship, and frankly, I didn't expect to find someone I cared for up here."

"It's all right, Darach. I understand you might not be able to deal with my past. I like you. I like that you didn't walk out last night when you could have done. I like the sensation of feeling your skin next to mine, of being in your arms, of you holding me. No one has ever simply held me, not even my mother. I used to hug Sadie when she had nightmares. Mum would usually be too far gone to care, or out somewhere. Maybe I should feel more sexy than safe in your arms, but you made me feel both, and you didn't reject me, even after I pushed hard to make you. I can't change the past and I can't change this." He glanced down at his body.

"Do you still want it? The pain?"

"There are times when I want it. I could get away from myself then. Clear my mind of everything and concentrate on the pain. It helped me to deal with losing her, and at least if he had me, no other poor sod had to be hurt to fulfill his sadistic tendencies."

"Oh hell, Brice."

In the darkness, arms wrapped around him and hands touched his back. More than anything he was desperate to be touched. He let himself be hugged until Darach moved away. A soft head butted against his back.

"It's all right, Princess. Daddy is fine." She purred loudly and settled down on the pillow above his head. Brice saw Darach's smile in the darkness.

"She's the reason I found you. She was meowing on the wall outside, so I followed her and found you. I think she deserves something special for breakfast."

"Bacon for everyone, then."

"I have to get up," Darach said. "I'm working today and the snow was coming down heavily last night." He swung his legs over the edge of the bed, giving Brice a view of his strong back and round arse. He leaned over and placed a gentle kiss in the hollow above the crack.

Darach turned his head. "Those things on the windowsill?"

"They belonged to my sister. She loved them, the gonks, trolls and My Little Ponies. I'd get them for her whenever I found one. I keep them here to remind me, along with her photograph. It's the only one I have. We had a party for her eighth birthday, just before she was… I nicked a cake and nearly got caught. Luckily, I could run faster than the shop owner."

Brice used the hanging handle to lever himself into his chair. Darach's face showed only concern. He glanced at Sadie's photograph and swallowed hard to push back the tears.

"My therapist helped me to deal with everything. I've been seeing her for over two years. I don't want your pity, Darach. I don't want you to think of me as some damaged, fragile creature. Maybe I was at one time, but I've worked hard to value myself and, with Alisha's help, I've learned to live with the choices I've made, so in that spirit — fancy joining me in the shower? There's plenty of room for both of us. And my seat is exactly the right height for me to give you the best blow job you've ever had, if your dick has recovered enough, old man."

A grin spread across Darach's face. "I'll give you 'old man'. I'm not thirty for a few weeks yet. And my cock is showing every sign of recovery now that it has been given the right incentive."

Brice wheeled himself forward a few feet, allowing Darach to come up behind him. "If you push me, we'll get there faster."

Darach didn't need telling twice as they flew out of the room to the bathroom.

"You'll have to stand closer to me to get the water on you," Brice said, tearing his gaze away from scrutinizing the erection waving in front of him.

Darach moved forward. "Is that better?" he asked, peering down.

Brice stuck out his tongue and licked around the tip of Darach's cock, tasting the bitterness of pre-cum on the back of his tongue. He turned on the water, shivering until it warmed up, then briefly turned his face upward to allow the water to flow over his face before he returned his attention to the several inches of manly goodness in front of him. He grabbed hold of the base of Darach's cock with his hand then moved his head forward to encase the rest, gratified to hear Darach gasp.

"Feels good." Darach leaned forward, pressing his palms to the tiles above Brice's head. Brice had no problem taking Darach deeper, but instead, he pulled in his cheeks and sucked harder while using his hand to stroke up and down, listening to Darach breathing harder and moaning above him.

"Bloody hell, you're good at this. Your mouth has more suction power than a hoover."

Brice was tempted to pull off and ask Darach how he knew, but instead, he reached down to his own cock, glad for his own swift powers of recovery.

"I'm going to come," Darach warned.

Brice pulled away, not prepared to swallow yet. He kept pumping until Darach threw back his head and splashed streams of cum all over his chest, watching as the water washed it away. A few pulls on his own cock sent him over the edge as well.

"I'm not sure I can cope with starting each day with two orgasms," Darach said. "I feel wobbly. Maybe I am getting old after all. We'd better have a wash. Can I do your hair?"

The feel of fingers running over his head soothed him. "Mmm, that would be good," he said. "The shampoo is there."

* * * *

Half an hour later, they were washed, dried, dressed and in the kitchen. Brice put several pieces of bacon on the grill and buttered four slices of Maggie's multi-seeded bread.

"I should be able to get out later," Darach said from the doorstep. "I've removed the snow from the top of the car and the windscreen. Bloody hell, that bacon smells good. I'll put the kettle on."

Sitting at the kitchen table, Brice pondered the situation. "We'll have to tell your inspector we're in a relationship. Are you all right with him knowing?" He couldn't ask his real question—the one about where they went from there.

"I'll see him today. I might not be able to get back tonight, although the forecast says this is winter's last blast. If you want me to come back, that is."

Brice did a double take. Was Darach as uncertain as he was? "Come back when you can. I've liked having you here, waking up with you. I've been on my own a while and, well, before wasn't exactly..."

Darach put a hand over his. "I know, and I need to take things slowly as well. How d'you fancy visiting Duff House to see the collection? They have a lot of Scottish paintings, or maybe you've been?"

"No, I'd love to go. My therapist says I should get out more and the gallery would be great as long as I can get in. To tell you the truth, I haven't been anywhere around here."

"Then the world is our oyster. I'll check, but I'm sure they have a lift. I went to a wedding there a few years back."

Darach bit a large chunk out of his bacon sandwich. "Hmm, exactly how I like it."

Brice smiled around his own mouthful of salty goodness. He could easily get used to this.

Chapter Twelve

Darach's stomach rumbled. He'd missed breakfast in his hurry to get out for his date with Brice. If this was a date. "I'm starving. Do you want to have something in the café here, or do you want to get fish and chips and go down to the links? We could park and watch the sea or something."

They'd spent the last couple of hours wandering around the various exhibitions at Duff House.

"Take me to the beach," Brice said. Despite being so close, he hadn't been to the coast much, because it reminded him of things he could no longer do, like walking along the beach feeling the sand between his toes. Sand wasn't conducive to wheelchair use.

"Right, then, there's a place on the main street that does takeout." Darach pressed the button to summon the lift, and twenty minutes later, they were sitting watching a couple of dogs playing on the small sandy beach while their owners threw balls for them to fetch.

Darach opened the window. The breeze had died down but still had a chilly edge to it. "Not too cold for you?" he asked.

"No, and the food is keeping me warm. It's good to get some fresh air. My therapist was right. I do need to get out more. Oh, my God — look."

Darach followed the direction Brice was pointing.

"Dolphins," Brice said excitedly. "I've only seen them that one other time. There are a lot of them. Isn't it incredible the way they jump out of the water for the fun of it? They seem so free and without care the way they twist and turn. I suppose you've seen them lots before."

"A few times," Darach said. "But they never get boring. I've seen whales too, and there are seals down on the rocks past Buckie. You should go on a boat trip. I think there's one that starts trips at Easter — the *Seascape II* — and before you say anything, they will take people in wheelchairs. It's decided — we're going. Now, where else could we go?"

By the time they'd watched the dolphins disappear out of view and they'd eaten their food, Darach had come up with several ideas for places to visit. "I haven't been to many tourist spots myself."

"I suppose you don't when you live there anyway," Brice said.

"Exactly. And you'd be able to sketch as well and not simply rely on photographs from the net." He hadn't been this excited in years. It was like seeing his home area through new eyes and realizing it wasn't as dull as he remembered. He liked the thought of showing Brice around. Off duty in Glasgow, all he and Mitch had done was go out to eat or to the pub. They hadn't even been to the theater, and Mitch had yawned at any mention of a museum, favoring other activities like trips to the races at Hamilton and Musselburgh. Darach had loved the horses, but betting was a mug's game. The only people who won were the bookies, and sometimes he'd worried about how much Mitch had spent on those days out.

Brice turned to face him. "You seem close with your family. Why did you leave? From what Maggie said, your parents were supportive when you came out."

"I grew up on a farm, but I knew from early on that farming and working with livestock wasn't for me. Mum worked long hours as a vet, and Dad had to be up early and on hand for the animals. We didn't go on holiday because we couldn't leave. It was fun when I was young, but boring for a teenager. I let other things occupy my time then. One of the good things about being on a farm is the number of hidey-holes allowing some privacy, although the straw does get everywhere."

"Who was your first?" Brice asked.

"You remember the party?"

"Yeah, but I've met Tosh loads of times—he *is* my postman."

"No, not him—Gus' brother."

"The hot guy with the blond hair and beard who looks like he should be modeling underwear? I remember you saying something at the time. So how old were you?"

"I was fourteen and he was sixteen. I fancied him so much. I couldn't believe my luck when he dragged me into the cupboard in the PE department after we'd won a school's cup game. I ended up on my knees with his cock in my mouth, giving him a bad blow job among the PE equipment. We ended up doing the same after every game. He'd come down my throat once a week for nearly two years and warn me to tell no one what we'd done until he went off to university. He ignored me in the corridors and I said nothing—not even to Tosh. What about you?" As soon as he'd said it, Darach wished he hadn't.

"It's okay—it wasn't some scuzzy guy my mum brought home. Those came later. My first time was quite sweet. He was a couple of years older than me, but we fucked each other, virgins both of us. It was the one and only time I've ever fucked without a condom. I lied to Tommy and told him he needed to use one just in case. He knew my past, but I knew I was clean. Him I wasn't so sure about."

"I'm glad your first time was all right." Darach placed a hand on Brice's arm.

"Me too. He died a year later. They found him when he was seventeen in an abandoned house with a needle stuck in his arm." Brice lifted his head and gazed at Darach. "Drive us home, Darach. I want you to take me to bed."

"What?" Darach spluttered out the water he'd been in the middle of drinking. "Are you sure?" he asked. "We don't have to."

"For fuck's sake, Darach. I'm not made of glass. I want you to take me to bed and fuck me. Clear enough for you, or do you want me to draw you a diagram? I could if you wanted."

Darach's cock swelled in his trousers. He reached over and stroked the bulge in Brice's jeans, then pulled away. "We'd better get going, then, but I'm not saying no to the drawings."

* * * *

"I won't break, you know." Brice lay on his back, gazing up at Darach.

"I know... It's just... I don't know how to explain it. I think I feel a little intimidated."

Within minutes of getting into the house, they'd ended up naked with Darach kneeling between Brice's legs. Darach had placed kisses along Brice's jaw, sucked on his lower lip and traced the trail of ivy as it wove its way across Brice's chest, down his abdomen and around his left hip. Each kiss along the way had brought moans, especially when he'd made the occasional nip and licked around each pierced nipple.

"Is it the tattoos, the piercings, or the fact that my legs don't work bothering you? You don't have to worry that you might hurt me. Lie on your back next to me."

Darach did as he was told. Brice lifted Darach's arm, turned on his side and propped his head up. He placed his thumb and finger at either side of one nipple, sending shivers down Darach's spine when he slowly squeezed.

"Oh hell, feels so good."

Brice reached across and tweaked the other nipple, making Darach want to push upward. He leaned over and enclosed Darach's other nipple between his lips then began to suck then lick, then bite, then more tongue, over and over until Darach squirmed under his touch.

"Shit. Oww." Pain shot through his sensitized nub. Brice stopped. "Too much?" he asked.

"Yes, no, I don't know. Oh God, you are so not fair." Brice

had begun to lick again and sucked on the engorged nub as if his life depended on it. Heat pooled in Darach's belly — heat and desire. His cock stood at attention, dripping clear liquid onto his stomach. Brice stopped tweaking his other nipple and allowed his fingers to move slowly down Darach's body. Ignoring the blatantly demanding cock, Brice clasped each of Darach's balls in turn and rolled them across his palm. Darach lurched up, unable to stop himself.

"Oh, fuck." Brice let go and spat on his fingers.

"Your wish is my command. Lift your leg." Darach did as he was told, allowing Brice to put his arm underneath. Brice pushed a finger at Darach's hole, and he instinctively moved his legs apart. The finger demanded entrance, pushing against and breaching the sphincter muscle, slowly moving forward then pulling back.

"Sit up a little. I want to suck your dick."

Darach did as he'd been told and lifted himself slowly so Brice's finger remained in his arse. He wanted both. Brice glanced at him, grinning before he enclosed the tip of Darach's cock between his swollen lips and sucked in his cheeks, pushing his tongue into his slit then swirling it around the head. He had no idea how Brice could do it all — lick and suck and fuck. He allowed himself to get lost in the rhythm until the first tingling sensations indicating the start of his orgasm began.

"Stop or I'm going to come. I thought you wanted me to fuck you."

Brice pulled away and gazed at him, the blue of his eyes almost nonexistent and replaced by black. "I do. I was getting you started. I want to be on my back. I want to see you."

And I don't have to see your back that way. "All right, you lie down. Lube and condoms?" he asked.

"In the top drawer. You'll need to prep me, but I've been practicing."

Darach opened the top drawer and saw the butt plug lying next to the other supplies. "So I see. Oh wow, it has a remote control as well." Maybe he could get Brice to let him try using it. There was something so spine-tingling about the idea of giving Brice the controls while his cock was being sucked.

Brice sniggered. "Maybe you'd like to try it some time. Imagine being fully dressed with a plug in your arse and me being able to make it vibrate at any time. Imagine how much you'd want to be fucked, how hard your cock would be, how I could make it go, and stop and go."

Darach grabbed the lube and slathered it on his fingers then pushed one then two into Brice's willing arse. After a minute or two, he found Brice's prostate and began to move over it, to and fro.

"So good," Brice said. "So damn good. Enough, though. Fuck me."

Darach wanted to ask if he was sure again, but was afraid Brice would think he was patronizing him because of his condition. Instead, he positioned himself, kneeling between Brice's legs and lifting them over his thighs. He rolled the condom onto his cock, applied more lube, then lined himself up. Brice put a hand on each side of his body and pushed down so Darach entered more quickly and found himself finally balls deep.

"Fuck me," Brice said. "I told you I'm not made of glass. Make me feel it. Make me remember my arse has been full of you."

For a moment, Darach closed his eyes and sucked in a large breath. He withdrew, but not fully, before he pushed back in, hoping he had the right angle to hit Brice's prostate every time.

"You are so beautiful," he said, staring down. "Your arse feels wonderful around my cock. I don't think this is going to take long. You might want to grab your cock and give it some encouragement."

Brice didn't need to be asked twice. He reached down and worked the pre-cum down and up. The muscles around his cock tightened and Brice's whole body pulled up, as if trying to get away from him. He pushed forward again. Brice clutched at the sheets with his free hand and came, sending streams of hot white liquid over his narrow chest and tremors through his arse. Darach had no choice but to follow as those muscles clenched around him and he pumped himself into the condom before almost falling down on Brice. Instead, he clasped the condom, lifted Brice's leg and rolled to one side, placing the used condom in the bin he'd seen at the side of the bed. Both lay there breathing heavily. Darach reached again and grabbed a wodge of tissues from the box, then wiped the cum from Brice.

"Thank you," Brice said.

"You're welcome," Darach replied.

"No, thank you for fucking me like you meant it."

Darach sat up, not sure of Brice's words. "I did mean it. I wanted to fuck you."

"I know. You treated me like you wanted *me*, not simply a boy-toy twink you could shag and leave and not give a damn, but you didn't treat me like I'd break either."

Darach leaned over and kissed him, pulling Brice forward and deliberately putting his hand on Brice's back. "I can't not know these are here. I can't not know about your past. I can't not worry whether you want something more from me, something I might not be able to give…"

"But—" Brice interrupted.

"But I want to see where we go with this. There are things we both need to explore and find out about each other. There are aspects of myself I've never explored and maybe… I mean, I'm not saying… Oh, hell."

Brice kissed his nose. "Stop stressing, agonizing about what you think I want. I can feel good without the pain. I've done a lot of research since I came here, for when I had my therapy sessions, and I know what Tommy did to me had nothing to do with BDSM or any initials you'd like to use. I didn't crave the pain for the right reasons either. I didn't know anything but my life with him for too many years. I thought I had what I wanted. I've learned since that I was mistaken, but it took me a while. Alisha, my therapist, doesn't let me get away with any bullshit. She explained how Tommy should have treated me, how he twisted everything to control me. She's been a lifesaver, so don't worry. If I want something, I'll tell you, and if you…" He winked at Darach. "Maybe I should put you over my lap with your cock between my legs and spank your arse until it's red and shiny."

Darach shivered. He had no idea if fear or excitement caused it.

Brice bit into his chest hard enough to leave a mark, then he soothed it with his tongue. "Something to remember me by," he said.

"As if I'm going to forget. Just one thing — no teeth on my cock, all right?"

"We'll see," Brice replied, winking.

A plaintive meow sounded on the other side of the door, followed by scratching. "I don't know about you but sex in the afternoon makes me hungry. I've the makings for pizza and salad and the boxset of the first series of *Black Sails* — lots of handsome pirates."

The scratching began again.

"Better feed her as well," Brice said. "Will you stay tonight?"

"I'll have to leave early in the morning if I do."

"That's okay, I'm an early riser."

Darach raised his eyebrows at the obvious innuendo. "I like to rise early myself. We'd better put the alarm on earlier than usual and try your shower again."

Brice grinned once more. Darach loved the dimples those grins created. He fanned his face with his hand.

"Saving water — very eco-friendly. I like the way you think, Darach McNaughton."

Chapter Thirteen

Brice wheeled himself the hundred or so yards from his house to the café. The sun shone, giving warmth for the first time as spring began to make itself felt, even up in Northern Scotland. Crocuses gave the borders along the hedges a splash of color. Soon the trees would blossom and regain their leaves and the birds and animals would begin their courtships once more.

Shit, I sound like a romantic idiot. But he couldn't stop himself smiling, or the pool of warmth forming in his chest at the thought of meeting Darach for lunch, or the memory of the night before. Darach had taken to staying over if he could. Last night, they'd spent the evening binge watching *The West Wing* and making out on the sofa. Never had Brice been more pleased that he'd chosen one in leather.

He pushed open the door to the café, waved to Maggie and Mel and rolled to the table in the corner near the window. Maggie brought him over a mug of coffee and Princess, who'd been curled asleep in the window, lifted her head, blinked at him then stretched before she curled around again.

"She's been here for an hour," Maggie said, handing over the mug.

"I've been working. I think she got bored trying to make me notice her. Not to mention she gets to lie in the sun here. It's a pity I haven't any south-facing windows with such wide sills like these."

"I assume Darach is joining you, as you've chosen a table."

"He texted me to say he was on his way, but couldn't stay long. He and Gus are giving a citizenship talk at the school this afternoon."

"Ah, he dearly loves community work."

"Really?" Brice wasn't sure if she was being sarcastic or not.

"Actually, yes. He thinks it's important to talk to kids as well as talking about being gay. He's done talks on sexuality for the force as well. Once he's certain of something, he's like a dog with a bone – totally committed."

Brice guessed Maggie was trying to tell him something, or reassure him, but he'd already begun to realize Darach was someone who didn't judge, but listened, wanting to understand. Darach read autobiographies of people from all aspects of life, he said, to discover why they'd made certain choices and try to find out what made them tick. He asked probing questions of Brice and he found himself sharing information about his past he'd only ever confessed to Alisha in their sessions.

The door swung open and the man himself walked in, crossed the room and, much to Brice's surprise, kissed him despite the fact that he was in uniform and there were a couple of other people in the room. He sat on the adjacent seat.

"Coffee please, Mags, and make it large. I've been doing paperwork for two hours. Have you ordered any food yet?" he asked Brice.

"No, not yet."

"I demand red meat," Darach said, winking at Brice. "Mags, do you have any steak?"

"Of course. A steak and onion baguette, then, is it? And the usual for you, Brice?"

"Yes, please, Maggie." He turned back to Darach. "I hear you're off to the school this afternoon."

"Yep, me and Gus. Oh, that reminds me." He turned to face the counter again. "Mel, Gus said he'd pick you up at seven tonight."

Mel's face brightened at this news.

"I've sent him to set up for us this afternoon. He said he

likes to drop in informally and chat to the kids in the yard before the more formal stuff. They've also set up an LGBT group in the school, so I've said to tell them I'd like to be involved as well."

Brice's heart wanted to leap out of his chest and wrap itself around the man next to him. "You know your halo is glowing, don't you?" he said.

"I believe in doing my bit, that's all. I've been lucky with my parents and my job. I want them to see that you can be gay and be proud of it. Maybe you could talk to them. I'll check it out with staff liaison."

Brice straightened in his chair. "What? You want me to tell them how not to do things?"

"No, but they might open up more to you. You don't have to tell them specific details. I bet the art department would love to get you in as well to show your stuff and inspire the students."

"Maybe. I'd be happier teaching art than spilling my guts about the gay stuff, but I'm not sure I'm the role model they'd want in a school with my hair and tattoos."

"I'll find out. You never know."

Maggie put their food in front of them. "I was wondering if you'd like to come round for dinner to ours one night," she said to Brice. "Mum and Dad want to meet you."

Brice glanced at Darach, unsure how to answer. Darach shook his head. "Don't blame me. I have nothing to do with this."

Brice thought for a moment. "I'd love to come, but will it be possible with the chair?" No point in mincing words.

"Darach is a big strong boy. There are a few steps to the door. I'm sure he could carry you, if you don't mind, and Rob could get your chair to stop it getting covered in mud. We've a downstairs loo as well, which has turn-around space, so you wouldn't have to go upstairs. We'd like you to come."

"In that case, thank you, I'd be pleased to have dinner."

"Good, I look forward to having you with us. Enjoy your

lunches."

Darach leaned toward him. "Are you sure? You know you're going to get questions, and no doubt be shown cute pics of me when I was little."

"Why d'you think I said yes? I can't wait to see those pics and hear all the embarrassing stories of things you got up to."

Red flushed across Darach's cheeks. "Oh God, this is going to be bad. I can feel it in my water."

* * * *

"Bloody hell. You look amazing." Brice smirked, especially when Darach moved his hands in front of his groin.

"Thank you, kind sir. I thought I'd treat myself to some new clothes." Brice continued to enjoy Darach's obvious discomfort.

"I don't think anyone expected you to wear a suit and the blue shirt matches your eyes perfectly."

Brice ran his fingers through his hair, pulling his fringe down into a point. He'd shaved the sides earlier with more care than recently. "The makeup isn't too much, is it? I don't want to show you up, but they may as well get the real me."

"It's only eyeliner. I think they'll cope. So, are you ready to go? Maggie's invited Mel and Gus as well."

Brice noticed a look of concern cross Darach's face. "Don't worry," he said. "I'll behave."

"No, it's not you. I'm worried about how Mum will be. She's going for tests in a few weeks—for Alzheimer's. She's been forgetting things—names, and to-do things—you know. It's hard for her. She's always been the life and soul of the family."

"It must be difficult for all of you."

Darach nodded and opened the door. "Come on, let's get this show on the road."

* * * *

Rob was waiting for them on the doorstep when they pulled up next to the front door. He introduced himself then grabbed the chair and bag from the back of the car and set the chair up again as soon as he walked into the hallway.

"You ready?" Darach asked before picking him up.

Brice braced himself and put his arms around Darach's neck. "Don't drop me in this mud, all right? It smells to high heaven. God only knows what's in it." Darach lifted him and carried him over the few steps before putting him in his chair. Brice checked the seat was secure and began to roll. Out of nowhere, two dogs appeared and danced around.

"Down." The reaction was instant as both dogs dropped to the floor at their master's voice.

"Sorry about them," Rob said. "They get excited by new people."

"You have them well trained," Brice observed. Both dogs lay awaiting further instructions. He held out his hand and Rob nodded, allowing them to come and sniff. "They'll be able to smell my cat, I expect," he said.

"Come on, the others are here already."

"How's Mum?" Darach asked.

"Okay tonight. You know, sometimes she's fine. That's the worst of it, when she knows she's not making sense, or she can't remember something. It upsets her and the rest of us, and it's only going to get worse. Life's a bitch sometimes."

"It sure is," Darach agreed.

Rob went off to the kitchen to help Maggie, leaving Darach to introduce Brice to his parents. Darach had obviously inherited his coloring from his mother, although he guessed her light brown hair was assisted now, but he favored his father in body shape and size. Stuart McNaughton had the appearance of a man who'd spent his life outside with his brown, swarthy skin and broad shoulders. He also had a firm grip when shaking hands. With his sleeves pushed back, Brice was able to see the tattoos on both the man's arms. Surprised, he glanced at Darach.

"Told you they wouldn't care about yours. Just don't start stripping off so you can compare. Dad had a misspent youth and ran away to sea for a few years before deciding to come back to farm after all."

Brice said hi to Mel and Gus, who were sitting on the sofa, then he turned to Darach's mother. "I brought you something," Brice said, handing over the bag. "I hope you like it."

Peggy McNaughton opened the box and pulled out the vase. He'd been experimenting with new glazes and patterns and this one was the first he'd been happy with.

"My, this is beautiful. Is this one you made? You have real talent." She examined the vase from every angle, running her fingers over the stripes of color. "Darach and Maggie told us you paint as well. It must be wonderful to be able to create. The most I've ever managed to do is knitting."

Brice shrugged. "Yes, but you can shove your hand up a cow and know what to look for, and I bet you've saved more than a few lives. I simply make pretty things."

"The world needs people like both of you," Stuart said.

Darach gave a slight nod in his father's direction then winked.

Maggie popped her head around the door. "Dinner will be ready in ten minutes, so if you could all go to the table."

Brice had no experience with eating around a table with a family. When his mother had managed to scrape together anything resembling a meal, they'd eaten on their laps. Food was never taken for granted in his childhood. He'd often gone hungry, giving his share to his sister. The simple joy of witnessing a normal family meal with the bickering and discussions among parents, children and siblings made him want to cry and laugh at the same time. These people he hardly knew had accepted him at their table without a second thought. They included him in their conversations and wanted to hear what he had to say about anything from the weather and its effects on the lambing season, to the reasons he'd become a vegetarian. Despite making a living from farming animals, none of them criticized his choice.

He listened as Peggy told stories of her days as a young female vet and how the old farmers had refused to accept that she could cope with the big animals until she'd saved a mare and her foal during a difficult birth.

"Nothing like saving the Duke's favorite horse to get you accepted by all and sundry," Stuart said. "We were invited to dinner with the family soon after. Now *there's* a place packed to the rafters with beautiful things. You'd love it," he said, turning to Brice. "But those things are seen by only the family. Unusual these days with so many big houses having to open to the public. I suppose the aristocracy doesn't get to keep their lives private these days."

"No, I suppose not." Brice couldn't feel it within himself to feel sorry for such people, having been brought up in a run-down tenement flat in the center of Edinburgh.

"Have you ever ridden?" Maggie asked.

"A horse?" Brice replied without thinking. A sharp elbow jabbed into his arm and he glanced to his side, not sure what he'd done. A few seconds later, the people at the table all burst into laughter, and Darach whispered in his ear.

"Sorry," he said, gazing around, embarrassed as heat rushed into his cheeks.

"It's all right, laddie. We're grown-ups here."

"But I wasn't... I didn't mean..." Brice said, spluttering. "Well, there weren't many horses in the center of Edinburgh, and since I moved here, well... I've never even considered it."

The blush on Maggie's face had receded. "I meant it seriously. Brice could get out in the countryside on horseback and see around the farm. He could use one of the horses from Cameron's stables especially trained to take commands through the reins. Darach, you could take him out. If you still remember how to ride."

"You don't forget, sis. It's like riding a bike." He winked

at Brice. "Or anything else for that matter. Would you like to come out with me when the weather is sunny? I promise I won't take you over anywhere too difficult. It does give you a different perspective and maybe we could go along the coastal path. You can't see all the little coves and beaches with only a car. There are lots of lovely isolated places, and horses don't tell tales."

Horseback riding was something Brice had never imagined doing. How would such an activity have been possible for a child such as him? "You say they're especially trained for the disabled, these horses? I suppose I could try a few lessons first to see what it's like."

"We've a horsebox so we could transport them and do a round trip somewhere," Maggie explained. "Burghead Beach to Findhorn is a lovely route if the tide is right. The feeling of freedom is wonderful. Galloping across stretches of sand with the wind in your face and hair and all that power between your legs under your total control." Brice heard a collective wistful sigh.

"I'll show you where I was conceived," Darach said, breaking the silence.

His father grinned and winked.

"Take a blanket, son. The bloody sand gets everywhere if you're not careful. It can be somewhat abrasive if you get it in the wrong place too, can't it, love?"

Darach's mother winced.

"It bloody well hurts, I'll tell you for nothing. Now, who's for a nightcap? Tea with a little added whiskey to keep you warm on the way home."

* * * *

The end of the evening came all too soon for Brice. Rob helped them outside and the others stood on the doorstep to wave them off.

"I think I'm in love with your family," he said as they drove away.

"I've been lucky," Darach agreed.

"Will you stay with me tonight?"

Darach chuckled in the darkness.

"What?" he asked.

"Has all the talk of riding given you ideas, then?" Darach asked, his voice lowered as he rolled out the word 'riding'.

"Maybe. But perhaps I should observe your riding skills first if you're going to teach me how to ride properly." The thought of having Darach impaled on his cock sent Brice's blood rushing south and the car felt decidedly warmer while the room in his trousers diminished.

The car's speed increased.

"Take your time," he said. "You're not on duty until the afternoon, and I want us both to arrive home in one piece."

Chapter Fourteen

Darach gazed down at Brice. "Forget-me-nots," he said when he identified another type of flower among the tattoos on Brice's chest. "The little blue ones."

Darach leaned over and kissed the patch of flowers under Brice's left nipple before licking the pink bud and sucking. He trailed kisses up to Brice's neck, following the ivy until he pressed his lips on Brice's for a few moments.

"Are you sure you want to do this?" Brice asked.

"What? Get filled up with you? I'm game if you are, but I don't want to hurt you."

"I told you I'm not made of glass, but I haven't…"

"Then it's something you and I can share for the first time, and I'm honored. Now get those fingers slicked up and inside me."

A while later, Darach eased himself down, making sure he didn't put his weight on the man underneath him as he straddled his narrow hips. Within seconds, he was full, having pushed past the pain. It had been over a year since he'd let Mitch fuck him. He edged those thoughts away.

"You can move, you know," Brice said, gazing up at him. "God, look at you, all muscle and brawn. You feel so hot and tight around my dick." Darach flexed his muscles, deliberately clenching around Brice before moving slowly up and down. Gradually, he sped up until Brice's moans filled the space, joined by his own as he corrected his angle so Brice's cock hit his prostate with every slide. Grabbing his cock, he began to work it with his hand until he knew he wasn't far off. He couldn't wait to see Brice's chest covered in his cum. His body tensed.

"Yes," he cried, sending streams of white liquid out over Brice's tattoos. His lover lurched up and shouted his own orgasm. Darach wondered if he'd ever get bored of seeing Brice's face when he came. He leaned down and kissed him then rolled off and lay next to him, still breathing heavily. Brice removed the condom and put it over the side of the bed. For a while, neither of them said anything.

"Are you all right?" Darach asked, piercing the silence.

Brice turned his head and stared at him. "I'm good. I think I might like to do that again. The heat, the feel of you convulsing around my dick. Your muscles are so strong. I wasn't sure if you were pushing me out or pulling me in. It must be amazing bareback. Other than that first time, I've never trusted anyone enough to let them…"

Darach sat up. "Are you saying you want us to be exclusive?"

"Is it too early to make those sorts of decisions? I know I'm clear of anything. I have to have an annual physical to check me over. I can show you the paperwork."

"I've never had sex without a condom."

"Not even with your ex?"

"No, Mitch cheated on me more than once. The last time was the final straw. I don't know, Brice. I'm not saying no, just not yet. Is that okay? It's nothing to do with your past. It's me." The disappointment flashed quickly across Brice's face, but Darach caught the look. Brice's Adam's apple bobbed up and down as he swallowed hard.

"It's all right. I shouldn't have said anything. Put it down to the heat of the moment. We'd better get some sleep."

Darach settled himself next to Brice. He didn't want to turn away in case Brice thought he was rejecting him, but Brice's declaration had thrown him. Did he trust Brice? He knew things about him, but what else was there in his past? No doubt Brice had sold himself to survive before getting involved with Tommy Mahon. Darach wanted this relationship to be different, but he wasn't prepared to rush into so huge a decision. He had feelings for Brice, but did those include love? He closed his eyes and waited for sleep to overwhelm him.

* * * *

The first time Brice fell off, Darach raced over and told him it didn't matter, but Brice insisted it was his own stupid fault and demanded to be placed back on the horse. Suzie displayed more patience than any animal should be expected to have over the several weeks of lessons.

During those weeks, they spent a lot of time getting to know each other better, both in and out of bed. Darach told him he wanted to be absolutely certain Brice could ride safely, and he passed the final test, a trip out around the farm, with flying colors. They planned a route for their first outing together along the beach at Burghead. Darach had called in a favor and the riding school had allowed Brice to take Suzie on the trip.

Brice watched as Darach and Rob put the special saddle on Suzie's back and added the saddlebags with food and water to Darach's saddle. He swallowed hard and gripped the arms of his chair.

I can do this. Darach will look after me.

He rolled the chair forward and patted Suzie's nose. She snorted, lifted her head, shook her mane then sniffed at his pocket. He removed a sugar lump and put it in the flat of his hand as he'd been taught, letting her soft, wet mouth take the treat from him.

"Everything okay?" Darach asked. "You've gone slightly pale. Not having second thoughts, are you?"

"I'm way past second," Brice said. "But I want to do this, and it'll only be a few hours. Will we have a phone signal out there?"

"Probably not, but if we're not here when Rob gets back with the box, then he'll raise the alarm. Everything will be fine. Let's get you on the horse."

He pushed Brice over the ramp to make it easier. Darach

manhandled him and finally Brice was fixed into place. He glanced down at his chair.

"I've never been anywhere without my wheels."

"I know, but we can't take it with us. You secure up there?"

"Yes," Brice said, wriggling a little to test his position. Darach mounted his horse and connected them together as a precaution so he could slow Brice's horse down if necessary.

"I'll be walking so don't worry. No galloping on the sands today. I'm not sure Suzie does above a trot anyway, love her."

Brice patted his horse's neck. "You take no notice of the silly man, girl."

Rob closed the box and came round to where the horses waited patiently. "Me or your dad will be back in four hours. Have fun and watch out for the sand." He winked as he climbed into the Range Rover. Brice watched him drive away.

This was it. He was on his own on the back of a horse. If he fell off, he would be stuck. If anything happened to Darach, he would be stuck. He gripped the reins tighter and leaned forward. "I'm depending on you, old girl."

Darach used his heels to encourage his horse to move and, at a slow pace, they made their way down onto the huge beach. A few other people walked dogs and there were a couple of paragliders out on the water. He breathed a sigh of relief, seeing they weren't alone on the sand. They strolled along, and Brice allowed his body to get into the swing of Suzie's movements.

Trees came right up to the edge of the beach at the back. The wind had dropped and the sun had burned off much of the morning haze. It was going to be a lovely day.

"It's my birthday at the end of next week," Darach said. "I'm going to be thirty. The family wants to throw a party, but I don't want one and anyway, I'd feel like the prodigal son or something. Tosh is having one at the community center. His birthday is the same day as mine. He's invited us. Will you come with me?"

"I'd love to, but we can't ignore your day."

"I thought we could stay overnight in Aberdeen next week and take in a show. *Hairspray* is touring. Would you like to go? I've checked and they have disabled access."

Brice gazed at him with twinkling eyes. "You have the tickets already, don't you?"

"I may have, and I've booked us into a posh hotel for the night. In the morning, we can go down to the beach and eat fish and chips on the promenade."

"Sounds lovely," Brice said, struggling to stop his emotions getting the better of him. No one had ever done something like this for him, and it wasn't even his birthday. Darach pulled up his horse and turned around, making sure Suzie had stopped as well.

"Are you okay?" he asked.

"I'm fine," Brice lied. When the hell had he become such a wuss?

"Have I railroaded you? We don't have to go. I only thought it would be something you haven't done before *and* something we could do together." He reached out a hand and put it on Brice's arm.

"It's lovely. I'm not used to someone doing nice things for me. I didn't get out much when I was with Tommy. And you want to be seen with me, even though I'm a tattooed cripple."

Darach stared at him, his eyes flashing with anger. His fingers grasped Brice's arm more tightly. "Don't ever use those disparaging words to describe yourself. Despite everything you've been through, you are the most beautiful man I've ever met. I want to show you the good things in life, all the fun we can have together, how proud I am of everything you've done and achieved. You have talent in every finger. I'm only a plod with no special skills whatsoever. You paint and make beautiful pieces of art. You've shown me there is beauty in the world — in

111

everything. After twelve years in the force, I'd forgotten."

Brice couldn't do anything but nod. Words escaped him. Obviously they both had their fair share of demons. For a while, they rode slowly across the beach without speaking. The only sounds came from the sea hitting the sand and whooshing back and forth, combined with the noises of seagulls as they swooped overhead. The sun warmed his back. He'd have to put on sun cream when they arrived at their destination across the bay. Darach had pointed out a group of rocks on the other side where they could dismount and sit leaning against the stones.

Brice hated needing so much help to get off the horse and settled onto the blanket, but they'd ended up laughing as Darach did his impromptu knight-in-shining-armor routine and swept him up into his arms then nearly dropped him again. Brice checked his phone. Thank goodness he had reception as he had some doubts about getting back on Suzie again.

After he'd seen to the horses, Darach fell beside him and grasped his hand while they both stared out at the sea and the clear, blue sky.

"Will you be able to behave yourself if I rub sun screen onto your body?" Darach asked.

Brice fluttered his eyelashes. "I don't know. Will you?"

Darach pulled his T-shirt over his head. "Maybe you should go first, then."

"Shit. That is so not fair. I burn with my pale skin. I bet you go all brown and sexy as fuck, don't you?"

Darach grinned, passed him the lotion and turned. Brice used both hands to rub Darach's back and shoulders. "Now your front," he whispered.

Darach lay on his back. Brice traced circles around each nipple. "Wouldn't want these to burn, now, would we?"

"But you could kiss them better," Darach replied.

Brice leaned over and placed a tiny kiss on the nearest, swiping it briefly with his tongue.

"Tease."

"Oh, you have no idea," Brice replied as he kissed down Darach's chest then tongued his belly button. Darach squirmed and Brice couldn't help noticing the growing bulge in his jeans. He reached a hand to undo the zipper, and less than a minute later, enclosed his mouth around Darach's cock, despite the other man's protest that someone might come along the beach.

"I'd better be quick and suck hard, then," Brice replied. He was as good as his word when a few minutes later, he swallowed every drop then tucked Darach back into his jeans as if nothing had taken place. Brice lay back listening to Darach pant.

"Has anyone ever told you that you have a wonderfully talented mouth just made for giving head?" Darach asked.

Memories rushed into Brice's head and he flinched.

'Such a good boy. That's it. Take it all. You know you love it. You're such a slut for my cock, aren't you? You have the perfect mouth for fucking. Don't move. That's it. Swallow it all. I don't want any mess on my floor. If there is, you'll lick it all, won't you?'

"Brice? What is it? Tell me."

Brice couldn't speak. He'd tried so hard to forget the hours he'd spent on his knees, the beatings he'd craved, his joy when Tommy had paid attention to him. For four years, he'd hardly talked to anyone. Tommy had been his world. Pleasing Tommy, because he owed him, and because he'd thought he'd loved him. Reaching out like a flower searching for the sun. When he'd witnessed the new boy trussed up like a turkey with Tommy fucking him, something inside him had snapped. The smirk on the boy's face, and the taunts about him being spoiled goods ready for the scrapheap. He clutched his chest, knowing panic would overwhelm him if he didn't breathe, and he curled his hand to tap his palm with his finger. *Concentrate on something else.*

"Brice. Brice. You're scaring me now."

He heard the worry in Darach's voice.

"Do you want something to drink? Should I phone for an ambulance?"

Brice grabbed Darach's arm and shook his head. "Panic attack — sorry. I need to get control and breathe."

Strong arms wrapped around him, dragging him up, surrounding him. "It's all right, Brice. I'm here. Nothing will hurt you. I won't let anyone hurt you ever again. Please be all right. You're safe. I love you and you're going to be safe. Whatever it is, I'm here for you." Darach's hand brushed through his hair and rubbed his back — kisses caressed his cheek and tears wetted his face.

"I'm fine, Darach. Stop fussing like a mother hen, will you?" Brice tried to process the words. Had Darach said he loved him?

"Are you sure? I'm sorry. What I said. It was stupid. I didn't think."

"It's all right. Bad memories. Sometimes I can't push them away. You can let me go now."

"Yeah, okay, you need some air. I'll get us something to drink and sort out the food. You must be hungry. I know I am."

"Yeah, food would be good."

Darach reached into the bag and removed the plastic boxes. Brice began to count backwards from one hundred, breathing in time with the numbers until he'd regained control. Darach placed the saddlebag next to him. He stared up into the man's big blue eyes. "I'm fine now. I used to be much worse. My therapist helped me learn how to cope. What you said reminded me of words said by someone else, and not in a complimentary way. It happens."

Darach slumped next to him and put his head in Brice's lap. "I should think before I open my mouth. Do you want to talk?"

"No, not about him."

"What about your sister? Is it too painful to talk about her?"

Brice stared out to sea. Sadie would have loved the beach.

She'd have run toward the waves, her long blonde hair flowing behind her as she'd dipped her toes into the water then run away again.

"I was eight when she was born. I didn't want a brother or sister, but there she was, this tiny little bundle. She didn't develop like other children because Mum hadn't given up the booze during her pregnancy. She'd managed to stay off the drugs, but said she had to do something. She didn't want Sadie either. Mum didn't know who Sadie's father was – too many possibilities. We didn't notice anything at first until Sadie didn't start talking normally. She never stopped moving and we thought she had ADHD. She would go up to people and babble at them. I used to read to her and she'd have nightmares where she'd imagine things coming to get her. I couldn't get her to understand what was real and what wasn't. She forgot things and, eventually, they said she had Fetal Alcohol Syndrome. Most babies with the condition are born with strange facial features, but she was one of the ones who wasn't. She'd go up to strangers, even though I told her not to.

"That day, I was late picking her up at the school gate. One minute she was there, then she'd gone. I was mad with the teachers, but when the kids are milling around, it's hard to keep an eye on all of them. It was my fault. I should have been there."

"You shouldn't be so hard on yourself, Brice. You were a teenager with problems of your own, and the man who abducted her was to blame. Things might have been different if the police had done a better job and hadn't simply accepted the evidence against the other bloke with no questions asked. There are so many ifs and buts. Come on, I'll rub sun screen into the bits that show and we can have something to eat."

Brice picked at the food Darach had brought. All the joy he'd experienced being on the horse, being with Darach, the sun on his back, had leached away like the water disappearing into the sand. He couldn't shake off his mood.

"I'll ring Rob and see if someone can bring the horsebox back early, shall I?"

Brice nodded. "I'm sorry. I've spoiled your day."

With some effort, Brice managed to get back on the ever-patient Suzie and they slowly made their way back along the beach. Brice stared straight ahead, hardly guiding Suzie at all, but she knew what to do. He guessed Darach had said something to his brother-in-law because Rob said nothing on the journey back to Brice's house where Darach had left his car.

Once they arrived at the house, Darach followed Brice into the kitchen. Back in his wheelchair, Brice felt secure again and in control. Princess purred around his feet and rubbed up against his legs as if he'd left her forever and there had been the distinct possibility that she might starve to death.

"Do you want me to go?" Darach asked quietly.

Brice wanted to scream out 'no' but somehow he couldn't get the word out. "I think that would be best. This isn't working out. I thought I could do this — be normal — have a relationship with someone normal."

"You can," Darach said, kneeling in front of him.

Brice shook his head. "It's too much. I can't..."

"I shouldn't have told you that I love you. I know it's too soon, and I don't want you to feel under any pressure. I opened my mouth and the words came tumbling out. Forget I said it. We can work on things."

Brice breathed in. He wanted to believe in Darach's words, but deep in his heart, he saw only the day when this lovely man would gaze at him and despise him for all he'd done, for all he'd allowed to happen to him. The marks of his past were there all over his body — a constant reminder. He might say the right words but... No, this was best. They needed a clean break now, before either of them fell any further.

"Too much water under the bridge. You've seen the dark side of people, Darach. You want to be the white knight on his steed come to save me from the bad things, but you can't. I *am* the bad thing."

"That's rubbish. Now you're feeling sorry for yourself."

Brice saw anger and hurt simmering just below the surface as Darach tried to keep control.

"Maybe, but you know deep in your heart I'm right. You're a good man, Darach McNaughton. Better than I deserve. Go find someone worthy of your love. Get married, have kids, whatever. You want to, don't you? You want it all. And I'm not the marrying kind. Please, go. I'll be fine."

Darach rose to his feet. "This isn't over. I'm going to walk away now, but this isn't the end. You love me, Brice Drummond, or whoever you are."

Brice desperately tried to stop the tears from falling. He grabbed the wheels of his chair and headed for the living room. "See yourself out," he said, before wheeling forward and not glancing back. The click of the door told him he was alone once again. He buried his head in his hands and wept.

Chapter Fifteen

Darach paced.

"You'll make a trench in the kitchen floor if you keep pacing to and fro."

Darach raised his head and stared at his friend. "I'm sorry. It's easier if I keep moving. I don't know what to do, Tosh. I thought we were getting somewhere, had something together, despite all that has happened to him."

"Remember I'm totally in the dark about his past. I know you can't tell me anything, but from what you've said, I'm guessing it's not good. Now, sit and eat this pie I've made from scratch. Harry will be on his way up in a minute. I texted him to let him know the food was ready."

"I'm sorry. It's good of him to get out of the way while I rant." Darach, finally sat at the table after he'd paced the floor for half an hour pouring his heart out.

"Did I do the wrong thing telling him that I love him?"

"That depends," Tosh replied, putting the plate of pie and vegetables in front of Darach. "Did you say it to make him feel better about himself, or because it's true? From the little you've told me, I'd guess no one has ever told him those words and he has no idea why you should have feelings for him. He might think you pitied him and wanted to make him feel better. I've been delivering his post for two years and we've exchanged words, but I wouldn't say I know him. He doesn't exactly give off welcoming vibes. You might be better off asking Harry to speak to him to see how the land lies. Harry admires his work. He says Brice could get lots of customers if he had his own website, but I suppose his past won't allow such publicity. He's here to hide, isn't he? That much seems obvious. No one moves to the Northeast Coast of Scotland without a reason."

Darach sighed. Tosh's expression told him his words applied to him as well as Brice. He hadn't told him what had happened with Mitch either.

"You can talk about him. I won't mind."

Darach nodded. "I know, Tosh, but part of me is embarrassed by what happened with Mitch. No one likes to admit they weren't enough for someone. It's still rather raw. I shouldn't have given him the first and second chances — once a cheat, always a cheat. I'm sure there were more than the three occasions I caught him, but the last one was in our bed, in our flat. The lad was barely eighteen. I'm not sure he'd even started shaving. I realized I couldn't compete. I thought we'd settle down, get a bigger house, have kids, even, but I was living in cloud cuckoo land. Then there was this case and…"

Harry came in through the door, interrupting his speech. He kissed Tosh and sat next to him, sniffing loudly. "This smells good, I love your steak and kidney pie."

He glanced at Darach over his glasses. "It's good to see you again. Tosh told me you'd broken up with Brice. That's a pity. He seemed so much happier when we met to discuss selling his work. I'm supposed to be going around there tomorrow before the party. I could try talking to him if you want. Maybe even persuade him to come. You're still coming, aren't you? Perhaps if you two met on neutral ground, you might be able to sort something out."

Tosh put his hand on Darach's arm. "It's worth a try, isn't it?"

"I suppose." Darach didn't feel particularly hopeful that Brice would agree to attend the event.

"Good. I'm closing early tomorrow and going over there to pick up three paintings and a batch of different colored bowls. I'll see what I can do."

They sat in silence for a while, eating the food. Darach wasn't in the mood for a party, but he could hardly miss

Tosh's thirtieth, and he had little interest in celebrating his own. He'd already called the hotel and canceled the reservations he'd made for him and Brice. He wanted his own thirtieth to pass without any fuss, despite Maggie's threat that she was going to make him a cake, whether he wanted one or not. He'd have a quiet night with his family instead of the time away he'd hoped for.

"Did you get your accounts sorted?" Tosh asked.

"Yes, and I'm making a small profit. I'll have to visit more auctions soon, though."

"Do you bid for most of your merchandise?" Darach asked.

"That and local craftsmen and women like Brice. You have to know what will sell, and how much to pay. It may appear as if I have a shop full of bric-a-brac but each piece has been carefully chosen."

"Except when you buy a box of stuff and have no idea what's in it," Tosh said. "Then we go off to the car boot sales."

Darach filled the time asking Harry questions about his work and what sort of pieces he stocked, keeping the conversation from himself. Tosh and Harry stayed close to each other—the small touches and glances between them told Darach all he needed to know about their relationship. Part of him was glad to see his friend so happy, but the little green god of jealousy couldn't be suppressed all the time. He wouldn't have ever put the two men together—Harry with his slim figure, tight suits, bow ties, balding head and pince-nez glasses and Tosh, laid back and easygoing, who liked a pint and watching the footie on a Saturday afternoon. But somehow they suited each other—maybe opposites did attract.

By ten, he was yawning. "I'd better get off. I'm on early shift tomorrow so I could come to your party. I'll see you both at seven."

Darach stood and made his way to the flat door. Tosh followed him downstairs. He opened the outside door and stood staring out into the night along the street to the single bungalow at the end of the row of buildings.

"Harry will talk to him tomorrow. He can be quite persuasive when he wants to be."

Darach hugged his friend. "I'm glad you're happy."

"I am. Harry may not be everyone's cup of tea, but he suits me, and I love him. I'll see you tomorrow night, and don't forget my present. No point in having a party if you don't get presents."

Darach grinned, climbed into his car and waved before setting off for home. He had no great hopes that Harry might succeed in at least getting them in the same room, but even a slim hope was better than nothing.

* * * *

"Damn." Darach swung his legs to the edge of the bed and reached for his phone. So much for grabbing a few hours' shut-eye before the party. He checked the name, saw it was Tosh and pressed the green button.

"Has Harry contacted you?" Darach could hear the concern in his friend's voice.

"No, I've heard nothing. What's up?"

"He said he was going to close at lunch and go to see Brice afterward. I got home at two, popped down to the hall and expected to find him here when I came back. It's five o'clock. He's not answering his phone either. I thought I might run over and check on Brice, but I checked out of the window and his car isn't in the drive."

Darach rubbed his eyes, trying to focus on Tosh's words. "No, don't go on your own. I'll be there as soon as I can."

"Darach, there's something you're not telling me. Should I be worried? Is Harry in danger?"

"I don't know, Tosh. Stay put and I'll be there. I'm going to ring off now."

He immediately called the station then Gus. Dressing quickly, he left the house five minutes later and ignored the speed limits. Darach rang the bell of Tosh's flat and heard him thump down the stairs.

As soon as he opened the door, Tosh made to cross the road.

"No, you go back. I'll wait for the uniforms to get here. Gus is coming as well." He put his hand on Tosh's arm.

"You're worried, aren't you? Shit, this is serious. Who is this guy? What did he do? You let Harry go and see him because you'd split up with him. You let him step into something dangerous. Selfish bastard. If anything has happened to him, I'll never forgive you."

"There's no reason to think anything has happened." Darach's words were as much to reassure himself as Tosh. "Maybe they've gone out somewhere in Brice's car and are out of signal range. They could have been caught in traffic or anything."

Tosh grabbed him. "What about accidents? Have you checked the traffic reports? They could have been in an accident and be lying at the side of a road, in a ditch. I could go upstairs and check the travel news."

Two cars pulled up—one a police car, the other Gus'. Three people jumped out. Darach quickly explained the situation then turned to Tosh. "You go up and check on those travel reports, but stay there. *Don't* come to find us."

"Now I'm even more worried. I want to come. He's my husband."

Darach didn't want to be harsh. "Tosh, do as I say. Go back to your flat. I'll leave PC Campbell with you."

Tosh nodded. "Okay, I'll go. Just let me know immediately when you find out anything."

Darach turned to the three PCs in front of him and explained the situation. "His car has gone, so this could be a waste of time, but we have to be sure nothing untoward has happened, considering the target's status. Don't put yourself at risk. Any sign of anything dangerous and we're out of there and calling for armed backup."

The three men swallowed and nodded. Darach led them

across the road and they took positions outside the house. Inside, nothing stirred but he noticed the curtains were closed. Darach motioned to Gus and they moved carefully to the rear of the house, down the side between it and the workshop. Darach nodded toward the open door of the side building and Gus moved to check it out.

"Nothing," he whispered.

The back door was shut. Darach crouched and, taking small steps, slowly pressed forward and pushed it open. Brice always locked it, even if he was in. Again, there was no sign of anyone moving inside. He beckoned to Gus and Moncur to follow him in and gasped. Chairs had been turned over and several bowls lay broken on the floor, but they didn't matter. He put out a hand to stop the others moving and compromising the scene any further.

"Call the station and get SOCO here. We need forensics immediately and the inspector will want to be informed." Pulling on a pair of plastic gloves he kept out of habit in his jacket pocket, he knelt next to the large, red stain. He had no doubt that it was blood – a lot of blood. Someone had been injured at the scene.

Gus came back into the room. "The team and the inspector are on their way." He nodded at the floor. "It doesn't look good, does it?"

"No, there's a lot of blood. I need to tell Tosh."

"I'll go," Gus said. "I know him as well, and you should be here. Do you have any idea who might have done this?"

"Some," Darach replied. It could only be something to do with Brice's past, and Harry had been caught in the crossfire. *Where are you, Brice? Are you all right? Think. Come on. Brice knew he might be in danger.* He braced his hand on the work surface to stop himself from shaking. *Focus. Falling apart won't help anyone.* A plaintive cry interrupted his thoughts, making them both jump.

"Shit! Princess." He rushed toward the sound coming from the bedroom. *If they've hurt you.*

At the door, he listened again, then, hearing another

meow, he moved swiftly to the other side of the bed and breathed out a sigh of relief when he spotted the cat crouched between the bed and the wall, her big eyes shining. He picked her up and checked her over.

"Thank goodness. Oh, Princess, where's your daddy? And is he okay? I'll leave you in here for now. Be a good girl, and I'll bring you food and a litter tray."

He managed to shut her in and went back to the kitchen.

"I'm going over to see Tosh," he said. "Moncur, secure the property and wait for the others to arrive. We have to follow the rules and do this properly." He turned to Gus. "I doubt there's much of this sort of thing to deal with around here. Come on, let's get this done."

When he walked around to the front, he could see Tosh standing in his open doorway, moving from foot to foot. PC Campbell stood by his side, preventing him from running over. He and Gus hurried across.

"Let's go upstairs," he said when they reached the shop.

"What is it?"

"Just go upstairs, Tosh."

He sent Campbell over to wait with Moncur, and he and Gus followed Tosh back up to the flat. He nodded at the kettle and Gus began to make tea.

"Darach, tell me. I'm shitting myself here."

"Sit down."

"Shit. Harry? He's all right, isn't he?"

Darach took the seat at the table next to his friend. "We didn't find anyone in the house, but there are signs of a disturbance."

"And...? There's something else, isn't there?"

"It might be nothing. We don't know the extent of the person's injuries, but there was blood at the scene."

Tosh put his hand to his mouth. "Oh, my God. Is it Harry? Has someone hurt him?"

"We don't know, Tosh. Neither Harry nor Brice was at the scene and Brice's wheelchair was gone as well. We don't know who was injured. It could be nothing. Harry could be fine. We've no reason to assume the worst. We have several cars out searching for Brice's vehicle, and we'll soon have people going door to door to see if anyone saw anything. The CCTV camera has been smashed, so we haven't got that to help us."

"But who? Who would want to harm either of them? Who the hell is Brice?"

"I can't tell you, Tosh. I'm sorry. I'm going to phone your parents. You shouldn't be on your own."

Tosh nodded. Tears dripped from his cheeks. "We've only been married a few months. What if he's dead? These people, are they dangerous?"

Darach didn't want to think that both men could be dead somewhere. "Gus, contact Tosh's family and explain."

Gus nodded, put the mugs of tea on the table and noted the number from Tosh's phone.

"I can't stay here, Tosh. I need to go back and help organize the door to door. PC Campbell will stay with you. Gus, come back over when you've contacted Tosh's parents." Darach hugged his old friend. "Keep your phone on and I'll contact you when I know anything."

He bounded down the stairs and ran across the road to his sister's café. Uniformed police officers were already knocking on doors farther down the street. He opened the door and Maggie moved quickly toward him.

"What the hell's going on, Darach? The place is crawling with police."

"Sit down, Mags. Can you keep this place open for us? We might need somewhere central while we're investigating."

"Of course I can. I'll put up the closed notice to keep out anyone else. But you haven't answered my question, and you're as white as a sheet and shaking."

"It's Brice and Harry, they've disappeared, and Brice's kitchen has signs of a struggle."

Maggie put her hand against her mouth. "But Harry was here at lunchtime. He picked up sandwiches and cakes to take to Brice."

Darach sat up. "What time, Mags? Can you remember what time?"

"A few minutes after twelve. I couldn't swear exactly how many. But why would anyone kidnap Brice and Harry?"

"I can't tell you, Mags. Harry's gotten caught up in something. I'll let my inspector know what you've told me as it gives us a timeline. It's four hours since Harry was there and they must have been taken soon after. Brice's car is gone as well. Have you or Mel seen anyone strange around today, or over the last few days?"

"There was a van," Mel said from behind the counter.

"Van?" Darach asked.

"Yeah, you remember, Maggie — the black one with the green writing on the side. It was in the street when we opened up and again when we closed a couple of days ago."

"Did you get a number plate, or what was written on the side?" Darach withdrew his notebook from his pocket.

"It was new. I think the writing mentioned engineers. We thought they might be surveyors or something for the road — you know, with the potholes."

Darach took out his phone and called in the information. "Gus is coming here," he said.

"What about Tosh?"

"He knows. I've told him to go to his parents'. We'll have people checking out the cameras on the roads all around the area. If they're heading back down south, they'll have used the A9 and there are plenty of cameras there."

Maggie grabbed his hand. "There's an accident on the A9 down near Stirling. They announced it on the radio a while ago. They may have been caught in the queue. They've closed the road and there are miles of tailbacks with the police attempting to divert people on to minor roads."

Darach stood wringing his hands when Gus came through the door. "Tosh's parents are on their way. SOCO have arrived and sealed the scene. There are tire tracks outside." Darach explained everything Maggie had told him.

"Should we go back to the station?" Gus asked. "The

inspector has called everyone in who isn't already on duty. Do you think they'll have taken Brice and Harry with them, back to where they are from?"

"I don't know. It depends whether they've killed them or not. We don't know their plans. They might have dumped them locally, or they could be taking them back to Glasgow. There are so many places you could hide someone around here."

"But they aren't local, and unless they had local information, they wouldn't know anything."

"Good point, Gus. We need to check on the local dealers. They must get their stuff from somewhere and *this* Edinburgh gang supplies dealers all over Scotland. Time to shake a few of the locals and see if anything falls out."

His phone rang. He listened to the information. Three eager faces stared at him, waiting for him to finish.

"They've spotted the van on the A9. They think it's in the traffic jam, but they'll need to organize an intervention. They're assuming the men are armed and there are lots of other cars and trucks in the queue. Somehow, they'll have to separate them. Hopefully, the gang will have Brice and Harry with them and it'll all work out. We can't do anything now. Gus, call in Moncur and Bryant and find out what they have."

"Strong tea all around, then," Maggie said.

Darach bit his fingernails, something he hadn't done for years. He hated being so helpless. "Please, Mags. Let's hope the next news is good news." He couldn't disguise the shake in his voice, and Maggie pulled his hand away from his mouth.

"Come with me," she said, dragging him toward the back of the café. "Mel, make tea for everyone."

Once in the stockroom, Maggie put her arms around him and hugged him tightly.

"It's no good me falling apart, Mags. I've got to stay focused. Only, what if? There was blood there, Mags, at the scene. We don't know whose yet. What if it's Brice's?"

"I guess something happened on your ride. Rob said you were both quiet on the way home."

"He told me he didn't want us to see each other. Harry went over there to talk to him for me. Shit, Mags if anything has happened to Harry, Tosh will never forgive me."

"But why would anyone come after Brice?"

"I suppose it'll all come out now. He's in witness protection, although it's a while since the case. His evidence sent down a gang leader in Edinburgh—nasty piece of work. We think someone from the gang may have come after him. He ended up in the chair after being beaten up and left for dead to stop him giving evidence before."

"Oh, Dar, I'm so sorry."

"What if he's dead already, Mags? And Harry? This is such a mess."

The door opened slowly and Gus put his head around it. "Sorry to interrupt, but the inspector is asking for you, Sergeant."

Darach wiped his eyes and drew himself up to his full height. "I'll be there now, Gus." He waited until the constable had left and turned back to his sister.

"I'd better find out what the inspector wants. I thought I'd left these sorts of cases back in Glasgow."

Maggie squeezed his hand before he pushed the door open and re-entered the café.

Chapter Sixteen

"Now you'll die like you should have done before."

Brice stared at Dean, not wanting to lower his gaze. Tommy's nephew had aged in the last two years. He'd had a habit of sampling the goods his uncle sold — both women and drugs. The last time Brice had seen his face had been when his boot had kicked him black and blue and he'd left him for dead in an Edinburgh alleyway.

So this was it. Brice shrugged and glanced at the well then back at Dean. He had little doubt that the walled water source would be his final resting place, unless someone realized he and Harry were gone.

Poor Tosh. Poor Harry. Why did you do it, Harry? They only wanted me.

Harry had tried to wrestle the gun from one of Dean's goons and had been knocked to the ground, hitting his head against the corner of the work surface as he fell. Harry was dead. There had been no rise and fall of his chest as he lay there on the kitchen floor with blood seeping out from the head wound and forming a crimson halo around him. They'd already thrown his body into the well and Brice expected to follow him soon. The big question was if they would shoot him first, or throw him in, knowing hypothermia could kill him, or the water would rise until tiredness overtook him and he'd drown. He sat in his chair and waited while Dean and his two minions discussed their plans. He needed to think — if he could keep Dean talking long enough and buy some time. His only hope was someone would check in the drawers and find his emergency documents. In the past, he'd doubted the police would care enough to make finding him a priority, but with Darach on the case, they might have people out searching for him. If Dean threw him into the well to leave him to die, there was a chance of being found. Brice realized he needed to ensure that this was Dean's choice. Above anything else, he wanted to see Darach again, at least to say goodbye.

Dean turned around and walked toward him with a smug grin on his face. "You did me a favor, you know, getting Tommy put behind bars. No one wants a queer for a leader, but now that he's dead, his death has to be avenged. It's only right. I have to show those around me that I'm stronger than he was and that I don't need to fuck pretty boys like you."

"Tommy wouldn't have let you near me," Brice said, sticking his chin out.

"Ah, but in the end, he didn't want you, either, did he? And you'd bought into his lies and let him do what he wanted to you."

Dean crouched in front of them, bringing their faces level. "I watched him beat you once. He had you tied up, hanging from a hook in the ceiling, and was using a cane across your back. I still remember the red stripes and the blood dripping down as you begged him for more. Finally, he fucked you, hard, not caring if the blood from your back smeared his chest. He'd always been handy with his fists, according to my dad, and a nasty bastard, but what I saw him do to you and the smile on his face when he did it chilled my bones, I can tell you. You did us all a favor, giving him an outlet for his sadistic tendencies, but he was my uncle and now he's dead, and he has to be avenged."

"What happened to him? Nothing nice, I hope. Nothing quick."

Dean's grin sent shivers through Brice's body.

He moved closer and whispered in Brice's ear, "No, nothing quick. I made sure of that."

Brice jerked his head back in surprise and glanced at the two other men leaning against the black van. "You?" he asked.

"Only in a roundabout way. Apparently, a little birdie gave the police evidence against a cousin of the girl who was killed by the same man who murdered your little sister, and he ended up in the same prison as Tommy. Somehow, he obtained a blade and a few minutes alone time with Tommy. By the time the screws got there, this bloke was wearing Tommy's balls as earrings. I'm sure you get the picture."

"So now you're cock of the walk."

"Yep, with Uncle Tommy gone and no chance of his return, I can run his businesses properly and tie up the loose ends. You're the last on my list, and thanks to my foolish grass in the Edinburgh police, I've finally tracked you down." He gazed around the open fields that overlooked the sea. "I have to say, there's some lovely scenery around here, but I can't imagine you get much of what Tommy gave you. Maybe I should get one of those two to give you a final send-off. Would you like that? Donny, he's the big bastard with the beard, isn't too particular where he sticks his dick, all nine inches of it. He won't care if you can't get it up anymore?"

Brice stayed quiet, trying to take in the information. Tommy was dead. Dean was now in charge and someone had revealed his whereabouts.

"So you have a source in the police, then? That would explain a few things."

"Another one like you — a fucking queer. Couldn't keep his dick to himself. Likes 'em young. Not that he realized how young until we presented him with the video and the boy's birth certificate. Useful having a cop in your pocket. When he offered you up in exchange, I could hardly believe my luck."

Darach would be gutted. The grass could only be his ex, corrupt and giving away information to scum like Dean.

"Now, as fun as it is to chat to you, I have things to do back in the capital. My girl and I are having a slap-up dinner tonight to celebrate my new position. I'm sure you'll have lots to think about while the water rises."

"So, I'm going in the well, then? You couldn't simply kill me and get it over with."

"Oh, yes. Did I not say? Bad me. I don't intend to dirty my hands dealing with you. This way any forensics are washed away, even if they do find you—from you and him." Dean nodded to the well. "His death was unfortunate, but he was stupid and in the wrong place at the wrong time. Now we're going to drop you in and take your chair and dump it somewhere." He turned and signaled to the two men leaning against the black transit van.

They walked forward, one carrying a rope, and tied it around Brice under his arms and around his body.

"How come you're not throwing me in?" Brice asked.

"We don't need to, and while you try to stay alive, you'll have time to think about everything you've lost. Our local source tells us the well is polluted by sea water. In a few hours, the tide will come in, the well will fill up and you'll drown. I'm told drowning is quite a pleasant way to go. Your legs are useless anyway so no point breaking them on the way down. A scrawny thing like you won't be able to keep himself going for long. We'll be well away by then with perfect alibis, should anyone suspect, and no evidence to tie us to you—perfect. The local plod won't have any idea where to find you, but we'll tell your mum both her children are gone if she's not off her head. It's only right she should know."

Brice clutched the chair and grimaced. He hadn't seen his mother since before the trial and hadn't any idea if she was alive or dead.

"Oh, she's still with us. Drinking herself to death still and trying to sell her body to pay for it. If the drink doesn't get her, HIV will. She's never been too careful with who she let have her. Practically selling herself for a drink when I saw her last tottering down the road. You must be so proud."

"Leave her out of this. Your family had her working the

street and hooked on drugs before she was sixteen. It's no wonder she became what she has."

"Enough of this chit-chat. Boys, dispose of him." The largest of the men picked Brice up easily and between them they lowered him down the narrow hole. At the bottom, a couple of feet of water already covered Harry's crumpled body. Unable to move, Brice ended up sitting on the man with his back to the rounded wall. The sound of running water told him the tide was coming in. A face leaned over the wall.

"I'm told it's best not to struggle, but I doubt you've any fight in you anyway." The rope dropped in after him. After a few minutes, the van roared away, leaving only the smell of its exhaust behind. Brice stared up at the small circle of sky the well afforded him. All he could do was hope that someone noticed Harry's absence as only Princess would care about his disappearance when she got hungry. Maybe then he might have a chance of being rescued. He could hold on for a while. Using a wheelchair strengthened his arm muscles, and he thought he'd be able to swim for longer than they anticipated, keeping his head above the water, but he couldn't stay afloat indefinitely. Now all he could do was wait, exactly like the last time he'd been facing death, and hope that somebody found him before exhaustion set in. Dean was right about one thing. It did give him time to think.

* * * *

Darach grabbed the phone when it rang. "Sergeant McNaughton."

"They've located the van in the traffic jam. It's going to take a while to organize."

His inspector sounded pissed off and Darach knew he'd have a lot of questions to answer. "I know, sir. They'll have to assume they are armed."

"They're planning to get the traffic off in front of them

and put unmarked cars behind and clear the other sides. An unmarked officer on a bike has eyes on the van now, but there's no sign of anyone other than the two men in the front. We've identified one of them as Dean Doherty, nephew of Tommy Mahon. The Glasgow force has now informed me that Mahon was murdered in prison last week, but the information hadn't been released to the papers, or to us, even though I'm supposed to be Drummond's liaison now. Bloody city cops think they know it all. This is a total fuck-up. Have you any idea how they might have located the target?"

Darach had, but he didn't want to believe Mitch could do this. "I'm not sure, sir, but I did talk to my ex-partner, Inspector Paul Mitchell."

"Personal or professional?"

"Personal, sir, but he's on the force in Edinburgh. He was involved with the murder case – the little girl."

"Could he have said anything?"

"It's possible. I didn't reveal Brice's location, but he was aware of mine, so I suppose Doherty could have found out from him." Darach didn't want to find out Mitch was the one who had turned him over to the gang.

"I'll check. You may as well stay where you are for now. As soon as we know how the operation went, I'll let you know. We also have people out searching for Drummond's car, but they could have dumped it anywhere on the way to the A9. There are lots of little places and forest paths we'll have to check. And, Darach..."

He noticed the inspector had used his name. "Yes, sir?"

"Whatever happens, we're going to have to discuss your involvement with Drummond."

"I understand, sir."

The phone went dead and Darach pressed the red button. Maggie put a mug of tea in front of him. "You should eat something."

"Not hungry."

"I couldn't help overhearing." Maggie wrapped her arms

around him.

"I couldn't bear..." He shook himself and swallowed hard. All they could do was wait to see if Brice and Harry were in the back of the van, and if they were still alive.

Gus appeared and sat on the chair adjacent to his. The two officers who'd been canvassing door to door had simply discovered the van had been seen on more than one occasion. No one had seen or heard anything that morning. Of course, it was possible that a tourist might have witnessed them leaving, but they could have loaded Harry and Brice behind the house. He'd sent the other officers back to headquarters.

"Am I allowed to ask who Brice really is?" Gus said.

"I imagine it will come out. His real name is Jimmy Boyden. He was a witness in the case against gang leader Tommy Mahon in Edinburgh two years ago. He was beaten and left for dead to stop him from giving evidence, but he did anyway. They put him here after he recovered under the witness protection scheme. My involvement may have caused this."

"What? How? I can't imagine you told them where he was, did you?"

"No, not exactly, but my ex may have done it. He was involved in the case." He sighed. "I don't know, Gus."

"You liked him, didn't you?"

"Brice told me to get lost because he'd only damage me. Ironic that it's my actions that could damage him. He might be dead already, and Harry as well. How the hell do I tell Tosh? He'll never forgive me. Those blood stains belong to someone, and I feel bad wanting it not to be Brice."

"We have to stay positive. Yes, there was blood at the scene, but it doesn't mean anyone is dead, and why would they kill Harry anyway?"

"They weren't expecting him to be there. If they didn't wear masks, he'd be able to identify them." His words hung in the air.

Darach sat in silence clutching his mug and waiting.

The minutes ticked by. He stared out of the window and watched the occasional car go by. He'd never felt more helpless in his life.

Chapter Seventeen

Ninety minutes and three coffees later, his phone rang—his inspector again. His hand shook so much that Darach struggled to press the right buttons. "Sergeant McNaughton."

"Sergeant, the men are in custody, but there was no one else in the van and the men aren't talking."

"Shit! Shit! Sorry, sir, but—"

"This isn't the time for this conversation, but I said we'd have to talk more about your relationship to one of the victims. I'm told you and one of the missing men are involved on an intimate basis."

Darach sighed. He supposed it was going to come out some time. "Yes, sir. I intended to inform you, but Brice and I split up a few days ago." Now it seemed like years since he'd seen Brice. "Did they find anything in the van? Signs of blood, or a struggle, or any other clues as to what might have happened?" Darach knew he was clutching at straws.

"The only item in the van was Mr. Drummond's wheelchair. We're checking it over now. SOCO have finished in the house. They said the cat was meowing a lot. Maybe you could check on it. Is there anything else you can think of that might help? I doubt we're going to get anything out of those three in the van."

"I can't think of anything. I'll deal with the cat, sir. Poor girl. I'll go and feed her. Brice loves his cat—spoils her rotten. Then PC Carmichael and I will check the local area. Do we have anything on his car yet?"

"We've narrowed the search area, but we don't have cameras everywhere and it wasn't fitted with a tracker. I've others out looking, but they could have been anywhere, left it anywhere along the route. I'm sorry I can't be more positive."

"I know, sir. I know my actions could get me into trouble but... I'm going to go over to the house then out while we still have enough light."

* * * *

Standing in the kitchen, Darach heard the plaintive cries from the bedroom. The room was covered with fingerprint powder. He doubted it would do any good. The blood stain remained on the floor. He gazed around and noted the blood on the corner of the unit. Had one of them been knocked over and hit their head? The placement of the blood suggested it wasn't Brice. In his chair, it was unlikely he'd be in the correct position to hit his head. Had they found any traces on the chair? He made a mental note to ring to find out. Gus came in, closing the door behind him.

"Do you know where he keeps the cat food?" he asked. "She sounds hungry."

"In the bottom cupboard over there. I'll go and see to her. Make sure you don't stand in anything. I know SOCO have finished, but we have to be careful."

Gus gave him a look that suggested he was talking out of his arse, so Darach left him to it.

He edged the bedroom door open slowly, not wanting to let Princess out of the bedroom. She cried while weaving around his legs. He sat on the bed and she jumped up next to him, nudging his elbow with his nose.

"Come here, girl," he said, picking her up. She settled into his arms. "I don't know where your daddy is, and I'm worried something bad may have happened."

Gus burst through the door. "I've found something." Seeing Princess jump down, he closed it behind him and put the bowl of food on the floor.

Darach stared at him. "Well? Are you going to keep me in

suspense and tell me or do I have to guess?"

"Sorry. I found this in the cutlery drawer. It's information about a tracking device."

"But there isn't one on his car. The inspector said that already."

"It's not on his car. It's on his chair. There's a special tracker on his chair. It gives a GPS signal exactly like a car."

"But we know they have the chair and he's not with them. It's useless." Darach resisted the desire to punch a wall or anything he could reach. Gus touched his shoulder and he glanced up.

"You're not thinking, sir." Darach couldn't help but be surprised by his constable addressing him as sir. Gus had proved to be forgetful when addressing his senior officer. "It may not tell us where he is now, Darach, but we can track where the chair has been and for how long and if it stayed in one place for any length of time."

He nodded. "If they stayed in one place for a while, it might be where they left them." His stomach churned. They could still be dead, but even the slimmest chance demanded investigation.

He jumped up. "Gus, I could hug you. Come on, let's see what we can find. We've still got hope now."

* * * *

It took twenty minutes to get the information using the number on the paperwork. The chair had stayed in one place for thirty minutes – a small, now abandoned farmstead out on the coast just over ten miles away.

"I'm going now, sir," Darach said, jumping into his car. The ambulance and fire service were on their way. He gazed up to the sky and offered up a quick prayer. Even if he wasn't sure he believed, it couldn't do any harm to try, could it?"

* * * *

The water had risen enough to take Brice off his feet. His arms ached and he glanced up at what he'd started to think of as his circle of life with an increasing amount of despair. Every so often, he'd lose his concentration and the taste of salt water would reach his mouth. He tried to move slowly, doing only enough to keep himself afloat. The water was cold, but so far had risen steadily rather than in a rush. Perhaps it wouldn't rise too far. He hoped Dean's informer had gotten it wrong.

A bird flew overhead, casting its shadow on his face. The sound of sheep and the tweeting of birds were the only noises he could hear. It was peaceful, soothing. He opened his eyes. Shit! He'd been going to sleep. *Must keep going. Darach will find me. I need to talk to him – to tell him.*

He moved his head, unsure whether he was finally hallucinating with the cold and exhaustion. Would a dying person hear things? He supposed it was possible. The wailing sounded louder now. There it was again, the sound of hope, the noise of a siren—some sort of emergency service. He wanted to shout 'down here' and wave, but instead, he kept up his steady breaststroke, hoping it wasn't his imagination telling him the sound was getting nearer. The car, its engines revving and tires turning, ran over the gravel left between the tufts of grass in the abandoned farmyard. Brice waited for the engine to die and began to shout.

"Help, help! Over here! In the well! I'm in the well!"

Suddenly the light above him lessened as a body leaned over the edge and stared down at him.

"Thank God, Brice. Hold on. I'm going to throw a rope down. Loop it around you."

"Not sure I can," he managed.

Darach disappeared. Brice could hear voices, but wasn't sure what was being said. The wailing became so loud it was impossible to hear anything else.

"Stay still, Mr. Drummond. I'm coming down to get you." The yellow-helmeted figure made his way down attached to a rope. He wrapped Brice in his strong arms and pulled him up, as if he weighed nothing, then he put another rope around him.

"Tired," he mumbled, clinging on as best he could. He closed his eyes and felt the rope being pulled, lifting him out of the water, and eventually over the edge of the well and onto the ground. Brice opened his eyes and reached around him, checking that he was back on dry land. His breath came too quickly and once again he was maneuvered until he was on his side. He dry-heaved while more strong arms held him and stroked his hair. Someone shouted his name as he threw up, his body shivering with cold.

"You're alive. Thank goodness. I thought I'd lost you."

Brice wanted to say something, but words refused to come. Once more, he was lifted and placed on a stretcher then on a trolley. A warm hand held onto his — Darach.

"You're going to be all right. I'm coming with you to the hospital."

He had to say something — something important. They had to know. Couldn't leave him there. "Harry."

"Don't talk. You should rest."

"Harry. In the well with me. Dead. Sorry. So sorry. Tell Tosh. So sorry."

"Oh God, no."

Brice drifted in and out, unable to understand much. People shouted at each other, then doors slammed behind him. Hands checked him over. The ambulance he was in began to move. He closed his eyes and everything went dark.

When he opened them again, all he could see was white. Machines beeped around him and an IV had been attached to his arm. At some point, his clothes had been removed and replaced with a hospital gown. Movement to his left made him turn his head.

"Darach," he croaked.

"Brice, don't move too much. You're okay. The doctors

have checked you over. No broken bones, only a few cuts and grazes. They had to raise your body temperature as quickly as possible to avoid you going into shock or developing hypothermia. It's a bloody miracle you survived. Other than that, you need to rest—properly rest. I guess the men who kidnapped you didn't realize how strong you were. You must have been keeping yourself afloat for hours."

"Using the chair...builds muscles."

"Don't talk. You swallowed sea water, though you threw most of it up again. Your throat will be sore."

"Harry?"

Darach sighed and squeezed his hand tighter. "They've removed his body from the well. My inspector has been round to tell Tosh. He's with his family now."

"Tried to help me. Hit his head."

"We know. The details can wait. Close your eyes. They're going to take you to a room soon and I'm not going anywhere."

"Good. So tired." Unable to stop them, he allowed his eyes to close again.

Darach stared at the man under the sheet for what might have been hours but, in reality, was just minutes. Medical staff came in and out of the room, checking Brice's vitals and replacing the IV. All he could think was that Brice was alive. When they'd reached the farm, he'd feared the worst. With no idea where to check and the cliff only yards away from the main farmhouse, Brice could have been anywhere, then he'd heard the voice coming from the well and everything had moved quickly and ended here, with him watching Brice's tattooed chest rising and falling steadily. For now, the detailed questions could wait. Brice was alive. For a moment, he thought of Tosh. Life was cruel—so cruel. At least they'd apprehended the bastards. Brice's testimony would put them behind bars and had finally put his past behind him as well.

Darach tried to ignore the niggling doubts in his head. Would Brice be allowed to stay? Would he want to stay?

Would he want to stay with Darach? Should he try to find Brice's mother? She was his only relative and should be here, but somehow he doubted Brice would want her there, not with all that had happened between them.

The room door opened.

"Darach? They said I could come in for a few minutes. I brought you a coffee and a sandwich — mine, not hospital rubbish."

"Thanks, sis. Take a seat."

"How is he?" Maggie asked.

"Amazing, considering what's happened. He's stronger than he looks." He gripped the chair arms, but failed to stop the shaking or the tears now streaming down his face. Maggie's warm arms enclosed him and he laid his head on her shoulder.

"It's all right, Dar. Let it out. He's alive. You found him in time."

"But what if I hadn't? What if he'd died in there all alone without knowing I loved him? So close. So close to losing him."

Maggie stroked his hair. "It's all over now. He's safe. He'll get better, and you'll be able to tell him how you feel. The pair of you need to talk and get everything out on the table. I'm sure he cares for you as well. I saw how he stared at you when he thought no one was looking. You can tell him Princess is safe as well. That'll make him feel better, knowing she's all right."

"Brice mentioned Harry when he was awake."

"Do you know what happened?"

"Theory is he tried to stop them and somehow was pushed and hit his head, and the blow killed him. Not sure we'll be able to get a murder verdict, but they'll be charged with manslaughter, attempted murder and kidnapping, so they'll be going away for lots of years. Police have raided their homes and collected evidence."

"Brice isn't going to like having to return to court. Gus filled me in on the details of what happened to him before. I remember reading everything to do with the case involving his sister. Such a tragic story and headline news for weeks both times. There are already reporters outside the hospital."

"Someone else can deal with them. The inspector will have a field day with the positive publicity of a murder case being solved, but he seems to be a decent bloke."

"You look shattered."

"I'll sleep in the chair. I'm not going to leave him. The circus will start soon enough, and I don't want him to face the media on his own."

Maggie patted his hand. "I'd better get back home and let everyone know you're okay. Some homecoming this has been. I bet you thought it would all be petty burglary and sheep rustling when you left Glasgow, didn't you?"

He stared up at her with heavy eyes and nodded. "I certainly didn't expect to be dealing with a kidnapping and murder, but then I didn't expect to fall in love with a tattooed man in a wheelchair either. Life has a strange way of fucking you up."

Maggie grinned as she opened the door. "It sure does."

Darach leaned back in the chair and pulled the other seat over, put his legs on it then closed his eyes.

Chapter Eighteen

"You're sure you're going to be all right if I leave you?"

Brice lay with his feet on the sofa and Princess spread across his lap. She hadn't left his side since Darach had brought her owner home a few hours earlier. She purred loudly as Brice stroked her head and back. "I'll be fine, and you have to go over there now. He's your best friend, and it's been three days since — "

"It wasn't your fault," Darach said.

"I know it wasn't, but it feels like it was. If I hadn't come here, Harry would still be alive. He tried to protect me and he was good to me. I didn't ever feel like he was judging me, despite my appearance. Harry had a kind heart behind his seemingly starchy exterior and those half-moon glasses, and he obviously adored Tosh. He positively gushed with excitement when Tosh agreed to marry him."

Darach sighed. "I didn't know him well. I should have come home for the wedding, but things weren't good with me and Mitch, and I couldn't face seeing Tosh happily married."

"Have you heard anything about what's happening with Mitch?" Brice stopped stroking Princess and touched Darach's arm.

"He confessed to telling them your location. They had pictures of him and an underage lad. He swears he had no idea the boy was only fifteen, but he's likely to face jail time, and that won't be fun, as he's a cop."

"No, I suppose not."

Darach rose from the chair, bent over and kissed Brice's forehead. "I'm not sure how long I'll be. I'll bring you back something from the café. You try to get some sleep, and if you need me, phone." He swallowed hard. This was going to be one of the toughest conversations he'd ever had.

Each step he made to reach Harry's shop weighed heavily on his heart and mind. Every time he lifted his foot and moved forward, his body wanted to turn and run the other way, but his steps took him closer and closer. For a few moments, he stood outside the glass door, staring at the closed sign. Some of Brice's brightly colored pottery stood on individually sized columns in the window. Darach guessed Tosh would sell up, so he'd be losing his home as well as his husband. Life could be a bastard.

He pushed open the door to the upstairs flat and trudged up the stairs. The sound of *Wind and Wuthering* by Genesis filtered through from the flat. Tosh loved the prog rock group even though he should have been too young to listen to them. Harry had shared this passion. Darach stood outside the flat door, took a deep breath and knocked loudly. The level of the music lessened. Tosh opened the door and, without saying anything, returned to his seat on the sofa. An empty tumbler sat on the table in front of him. Dressed in jeans and T-shirt, Tosh sat with his knees pulled up and his arms around them, his red eyes evidence of both crying and a lack of sleep.

"Have you eaten anything this morning?" Darach asked, even though he already knew the answer.

Tosh shook his head.

"I'm going to make us toast and tea."

Tosh nodded.

Ten minutes later, Darach placed the food and mugs of tea on the table in front of them and sat next to his friend. Not wanting to invade his space, he left a gap between them. He'd known Tosh all his life, but never had a gulf between them seemed so vast. Those few inches may as well have been the Grand Canyon. He waited.

"I put Marmite on yours," he said, finally breaking the awkward silence. "Even though I've no idea how you can eat such disgusting stuff." He held the plate up and was happy to see Tosh let go of his knees and reach out to take a piece. He bit a small chunk and chewed slowly. Darach lifted a slice to his own mouth and took a larger bite. In the background, the music changed from the instrumental into the introduction of *Afterglow*, Tosh's favorite track. The shaking began almost immediately and tears slipped out of Tosh's eyes and down his cheeks.

"We're going to play this at Harry's funeral," he whispered.

Darach opened his arms, and Tosh leaned forward. For the several minutes of the song, he sobbed into Darach's chest while Darach stroked his hair and held him close. Tosh spoke, but Darach couldn't make out the mumbled words until finally the sobbing was accompanied by Tosh's fists hitting his chest.

"It's not fair. Why my Harry? It's all his fault. You get to keep him, and I lose my husband because he tried to be a fucking hero. He didn't need to. It's so fucking pointless, dying like that. We only had two years — two years, Dar. It's nothing. I've never asked for much, but I loved him and his silly glasses and prissy ways. I loved him so much."

Darach continued stroking Tosh's back. "I know, I'm so sorry. If I hadn't..."

Tosh pulled back. Darach could hardly look him in the eyes.

"I'm sorry." Tosh wiped his eyes with his shirt. "I shouldn't have said that about Brice. It's not fair. I blamed you and him when I found out. When I heard what had happened, I swore I wouldn't ever talk to you again, but Mum and Dad said it wasn't your fault, or even Brice's. You didn't kill him. Those bastards did. I know they will end up in jail for what they did. He was in the wrong place at the wrong time. It's just that I don't know what to do now. Even this place seems so huge without him. There's the shop and his clothes and possessions. I can't face dealing with everything so soon, but I guess it's not going anywhere for now. Mum suggested I move back in with them. I don't want to stay here, but I don't want to see her face full of pity and have her fussing over me all the time either. I've decided one thing, though. I'm going to sell the shop and flat together."

Darach gazed at his friend, noting his eyes ringed with red and his slumped shoulders. "Don't make any big decisions yet, Tosh. Why don't you move into my house? You can stay there as long as you like. I'm not going to be there much. Brice needs to be taken care of, although, typically, he says he's fine."

"How is he *really*?"

"Recovering quickly. He's stronger than anyone might imagine. He's been through so much in his life."

"Any sign of his mother yet?"

"The police found her high as a kite. They told her, but how much she understood is open to question. Brice doesn't want to see her anyway."

"So, you and him?"

"I don't know. I'm not pushing anything."

"But you love him, don't you?"

Darach nodded. "I tried not to, but the thought of being without him, what might have happened." He stopped abruptly, realizing. "Shit. I'm sorry. I didn't think."

"Someone should be happy after all this. Don't let him go if you love him. I know there's lots you haven't told me, but I've seen the reports in the papers about his background and what that bastard excuse for a man did to him."

"He has this mass of scars on his back," Darach said quietly. "He let Mahon use him, wanted him to do it. I don't understand everything—not wanting pain like he did. He's told me some, but it's hard to get my head around everything."

"You have to talk to him, then. Let him explain, if he can. He may not be able to. We all have our needs and desires, and sometimes we don't understand what turns us on, what flicks a switch, when something turns from one thing to another—like you and me."

"But what if he wants me to…you know. I couldn't." He lifted his head and met Tosh's gaze. "I'm sorry, I'm supposed to be here helping you, not whining on about my problems. You know if you want anything, call me. And my offer of my house is there. I can help you pack what you need for a few days."

"That would be good. Can we go now? I'll sort out a few clothes. There's too much of him here."

"It's no problem. I'll drop you off there then get back to Brice. I said I'd take him some food before I go back to work. There's lots of paperwork to do, and we're still searching for the person who gave them the location of the farm, because someone did."

"I'll ask around. I still have friends who have friends. It would be good to do something to help. Oh, and is it all right if I let Sam know I'm at yours? He's coming over to discuss the funeral."

"Sam?" Darach asked.

"Yeah, you know, Sam Carmichael, Gus' brother. He's the minister at St. Mungo's Church. I thought you knew."

"Yes, of course. It's good to have someone you know officiating." He wondered how the church would view holding a funeral for an openly gay man.

"I'll get a few things together, then."

Tosh pulled himself up from the sofa and walked slowly to the bedroom. Fifteen minutes later, he emerged with a suitcase.

"Come on, then. Let's get you settled at mine. I'm glad you've let me do this for you." He pulled Tosh into a hug then led him downstairs.

* * * *

After settling Tosh in his house, Darach returned to work and began to make his way through the mass of paperwork on his desk. The reporters from the national papers had faded back to their Glasgow and London offices. Soon another incident would occupy them until the court case brought the event back into focus again. Darach triple-checked his and Brice's final statements, printed them out and made his way to the inspector's office. He waited after knocking on the door until the inspector shouted to come in.

"I've brought the complete statements, sir. Is there any news?" His inspector was a few months away from retirement and had been in the force for more than the minimum thirty years necessary to get one's pension.

"You can call me Ramsay, you know."

"Sorry, sir. Our inspector in Glasgow liked to keep things formal, and I forget."

"This is a small place. Everyone knows everyone's business, even if they don't always grass to us. We need to get the names of the dealers this Doherty character dealt with around here."

"I spoke to Tosh Mackintosh this morning. He said he'd ask around."

"How is he?"

"How you'd expect? At least he can plan the funeral, because we've locked up the guilty men, and have Brice's very detailed testimony. I've let him move into my house. Too many memories in his flat, and he's going to sell when he's ready."

"Thanks for these reports. Doherty and his men are being held on remand until the trial, which could be months from now. Is your man up for giving evidence again?"

Darach liked the sound of those words – his man. "He says he is. I think he wants to draw a line under the whole thing. About Inspector Mitchell, sir? Do you have any more information?"

"Bad business. He's been suspended and is likely to face charges. The Provost has yet to decide what they are, but he's likely to get a custodial sentence. He's let his dick ruin his life, but he wouldn't be the first cop to do that. Right, do you fancy getting out of here? We've had a report concerning sheep going missing out at Frazer's farm. Take young Gus and check, will you?"

Darach laughed. "Sorry, Ramsay." He managed to use his name this time. "It's just a conversation I had once about sheep rustling. I'll get Gus and go and have a look."

Throwing his coat on, Darach walked through the main office. "Gus, grab your jacket. We've a case of sheep stealing to investigate."

"Sheep? Really? I'll be with you now. It'll be good to get out of here and get some fresh air."

Darach texted Brice while he waited. Tonight, he wanted to talk about the future — their future.

* * * *

When he arrived home, Brice was asleep on the sofa with Princess lying on his side. He tiptoed across the room, trying not to wake Brice from his much-needed sleep.

"Bloody hell. What have you been doing? You stink. I can smell you from here."

"I thought you were asleep," Darach said, walking over and kissing Brice's forehead.

"I was until you woke Princess and she stuck her claws in my side. What have you been doing?"

"Investigating a case of sheep rustling, would you believe? I've left my boots outside. The farmer wanted us to give the place a once-over to see where he could improve security. Gus and I have tramped through goodness knows what today, and those sheep can be friendly buggers. Only the thought of a warm shower kept me going."

"I need a piss first." Brice moved into a sitting position, lowered the side of the sofa and maneuvered himself onto his temporary chair.

"I'll go and get undressed, then," Darach said.

When he walked into the wet room, Brice was brushing his teeth. He stopped when Darach appeared and whistled. Darach smiled and turned on the shower, waiting for the water to warm up.

"Are you going to simply sit there?" he asked Brice, who was making a meal of cleaning his teeth.

"I thought I might."

Darach stepped under the warm water and let it stream down his back and chest. He grabbed the shower gel and began to wash himself, deliberately exaggerating each squeeze of the sponge over his flesh. Brice's gaze followed his every movement, and Darach's cock stiffened under the careful scrutiny. He turned around and washed his arse. By now, Brice had rinsed his mouth and was concentrating his whole attention on Darach's actions. Turning again, he began to wash his cock and balls. Brice stared at his now completely stiff erection.

"Like what you see?" Darach said, stroking himself.

"What's not to like?"

"Should I continue?"

Brice licked his lips. "Don't let me stop you."

Darach grinned and continued stroking up and down, gradually increasing his speed until he experienced a familiar feeling in his balls. He leaned back against the wall and let the warm liquid squirt over his hand and down into the swirling water.

"Man, you are one sexy bastard," Brice said. "I'll be in bed when you've finished."

Darach tried to control his breathing as Brice wheeled himself out of the room. Ten minutes later, he padded into the bedroom and found Brice under the duvet with Princess curled at the bottom of the bed. He turned off the lamp and slipped under the covers behind Brice then put his arms around the smaller man.

"Feels good," Brice murmured.

Darach kissed the back of his neck and snuggled closer, smiling at Brice's tiny snores. In the dark, he couldn't see the scars, but he ran a finger across them, feeling each ridge. Would they be able to get over everything? That conversation would have to wait for tomorrow.

Chapter Nineteen

It felt strange to ask if anyone was home going into his own house, but he didn't want to enter without giving Tosh a warning of his arrival. "It's only me," he shouted as he stepped into the entrance hall.

"In here," Tosh shouted back.

Darach pushed open the door to the living room and stopped when he realized Tosh wasn't alone. He recognized the man from the party, although last time he hadn't been wearing a dog collar.

Tosh came in from the kitchen carrying a tray with three mugs. "I made you one," he said, putting the tray on the low table in front of the sofa.

Darach moved forward and shook Sam Carmichael's outstretched hand. "It's good to meet you again." He turned to face Tosh, noting the dark circles still obvious under his friend's eyes. "I can't stay long. I thought I'd pop in and make sure you were okay after last night, or if you wanted anything."

"I'm fine." Obviously, he wasn't. "I'm sure Mum will be round later with a stew or a steak pie. Sam's here to discuss the funeral arrangements."

Darach bit back an acerbic comment regarding the Church's position on burying queers. He recalled the old view of love the sinner, not the sin. His family weren't religious, but he knew Tosh's parents still attended. Maybe Harry had believed. It wasn't Darach's position to question.

"How's your friend?" Sam asked. "Brodie said you were taking care of him after what happened."

Darach had to think for a minute. He hadn't heard Tosh's

real name used for years. Even Tosh's parents called him Tosh. He'd been named Brodie after his mother's maiden name – Brodie James Mackintosh. "Yes, I am. He's recovering." He didn't want to talk about the circumstances with Tosh in the room. Darach still had his lover while they were here to discuss the funeral of Tosh's husband.

Darach found himself staring at the man he'd known as a teenager. Sam didn't share his brothers' bright red hair, being the only blond among them. Even so, the five of them together must make a formidable group. He was taller than Gus and bulkier. With the full beard, he had the look of an old-fashioned preacher, but his pale blue eyes had a softness about them when he glanced at Tosh. Darach hoped so anyway. Tosh had loved Harry, and Darach didn't want their love swept under the carpet by a zealous minister keen to erase the gay.

"We were discussing music," Tosh said. "I mentioned we're having the Genesis track. Harry loved *The Planet Suite* as well, especially *Jupiter* and the pop version *Joygiver* because that's what he brought into my life. I know he wore those silly glasses and seemed to peer down his nose at people, but he could laugh at himself as well. No one would have put us together, and yet we fitted somehow. I don't know what I'm going to do without him."

Darach felt like his heart would break as he watched the tears form in the corners of Tosh's eyes before he wiped them away. He was more surprised when Sam took hold of Tosh's hand.

"You told me Harry believed in heaven, or a sort of heaven, so hold on to that."

Darach swallowed a mouthful of tea, feeling like a spare part in the conversation. He stood. "I need to get to work. Let me know if there's anything I can do for you, Tosh. It was good to meet you again, Sam."

Closing the door behind him, he dismissed the uncharitable thought that had popped into his head. Had he always been such a cynic?

By the time he arrived home – yes, he was calling Brice's bungalow home now – some hours later, Darach had been unsuccessfully stifling his yawns for a while. He wanted a shower, food and Brice in his arms, though not necessarily in that order. He'd spoken to his old boss in Glasgow and discovered the charges brought against Mitch. He tried to remind himself that the man had done a lot of good in his career and had sent lots of bad guys down, but all he wanted to do was shake his ex and ask him why he'd been so stupid. If ever there was a man led by his dick, Mitch was that man.

Darach parked his car behind Brice's and noted the presence of his parents' Range Rover. He sighed. He loved his parents but… He fixed a smile on his face and prepared for their questions as he pushed open the front door.

When he entered the main room, Brice was sitting in his chair with Darach's mother in the armchair opposite. Princess lay curled on her lap. His mother glanced up, and he crossed the room to kiss her then Brice.

"It's lovely to see you, Mum," he said.

"You must be tired, Darach. I was telling Brice the pair of you should go on holiday somewhere. He's never been out of Scotland. You could go abroad or down south, somewhere different."

And away from here. Maybe his mum was right.

"I don't know, Mum. I'm not sure I've been here long enough for a holiday yet, but we can think about it, can't we? Is Dad in the kitchen? I'll go through and see him."

His father was taking a large pie out of the oven when he entered the room. Pans bubbled on the stove.

"Ah, Darach, you're in time to set the table. I've brought one of your favorites."

Darach sniffed the air. "Apple pie?"

"Your mother is worried you're both not eating enough. She thinks Brice needs building up."

Darach patted his father's shoulder and collected the cutlery and crockery from drawers and cupboards. He set the table. "How's she been?" he asked.

"Oh, you know, good and bad days. They're going to try a few treatments to see how things go. The worst is when she realizes she's forgetting things. I hate it when she cries. She couldn't remember the dogs' names yesterday."

"And how are you, Dad?"

"Oh, you know me, son. I'm trying to keep positive, but we both know things are going to get worse. She's written a list of the things she wants to do—a bucket list she calls it—which includes seeing you settled down, by the way."

Darach smiled. Of course her list would include that. "We'll see, Dad. I'll go and get them in."

They sat around the table eating and drinking while his mother went through her list.

"I'd love to go to Disney World too," Brice said. "Maybe we could go together as a family."

Darach glanced up at his father's face. "We could let these two watch the parades and go and have a drink," he said, smiling. "I'll investigate travel arrangements for your chair. You know what insurance companies can be like. Maybe for now we could do Disneyland, Paris. We could drive down and see a few places on the way, go through the Tunnel and have a look around Paris later in the year when the kids have gone back to school in September. What do you think?"

"Sounds wonderful," Brice said. "I'd love to see the galleries and museums, to be able to stare at the Mona Lisa or Monet's masterpieces."

"We'll do that, then," his mother said. "Brice told me he's going to set up a website to sell his work now that he doesn't have to hide anymore."

"Really?" Darach said. "More people should be able to own such wonderful pieces of art." He groaned while letting the beef melt on his tongue. "Dad, this pie is magnificent."

"I put a few other meals in your freezer. I told you that your mother thought you needed feeding. Now eat up because we have to get back home and leave these two alone. I'm sure you had plans other than entertaining your parents."

Darach's cheeks flushed with heat. "I may have done," he admitted.

* * * *

An hour later, he waved his parents off and returned to the kitchen. "Leave the washing up," he said.

Brice glanced at him. "You've your serious face on. Should I be worried?"

"I want a shower and yes, we do have to talk. I've been thinking."

"I'm not sure I like the sound of that." Brice gripped his chair harder, and Darach closed the space between them. He lifted Brice's head with one finger under his chin and kissed his mouth gently. "I love you and I'm not going anywhere, but there are things I need to talk about — things best discussed in bed with you in my arms. You go and get sorted and I'll be through after I've had a shower."

"Okay, but don't be too long, all right?"

Waves of worry emanated from his lover. He understood. Darach wanted to at least understand what had happened in Brice's past and what Brice expected from him. If they had a future together, they had to get over the past first, with all secrets out in the open and all skeletons out of the cupboards.

When Darach entered the bedroom, Brice lay with his back to the headboard, holding Princess in the air — she didn't appear pleased. He didn't notice Darach at first while he whispered to Princess, telling her how beautiful she was surrounded by the yellow bedding with chintzy flowers. To the side, on the shelf, stood his sister's collection of trolls with their colorful hair. It presented an odd image — the cat, the toys and the half-naked man with the tattoos, hair shaved at the sides and longer on top.

"Are you going to stand there staring?" Brice asked,

putting Princess down on the bed. "Or are you going to come in here and tell me what's on your mind before I go out of mine? Princess is a good listener, but she's not so shit hot at giving advice."

With a flick of her tail, suggesting Brice was underestimating her skills, the cat jumped off the bed and headed, tail held high, out of the door. Darach crossed the floor and lifted the covers then slipped into the bed next to Brice. He pulled the light cord hanging from the ceiling and plunged the room into darkness before positioning himself so Brice could lie in his arms with his head on Darach's chest. For several minutes, neither of them said anything. Brice reached over and stroked the hair on Darach's chest. Darach knew he was waiting, but even though he'd rehearsed these words over and over again, he hesitated.

"If I had to guess, I'd say you wanted to get everything out there so we have no secrets. Am I right?"

"I want to understand," Darach said. "I want to understand why you let him do those things to you — why you wanted him to hurt you. I know what you've told me about your sister, but..." Darach ran his hand over Brice's scars. "This is extreme. I thought Doms were supposed to take care of subs and their wounds."

"Been reading up, have you?"

"I may have been. I want to — Ow."

Brice pinched Darach's nipple then licked his finger and ran it over the hardening nub. Darach felt his cock rise in response and shifted position. Brice moved his hand, stroking him.

"See? The body might be saying something hurts, but sometimes the hurt is good."

Darach groaned again as Brice licked around his nipple then bit and sucked hard enough to leave a mark.

"Doesn't everyone like some pain? That bite that leaves a mark? The tug on the nipple between teeth? Like a tattoo — something beautiful and meaningful, but not achieved without pain. Look at women giving birth. For some, there's so much pain, but it's forgotten in an instant when they have that baby in their arms. Within joy, there can be pain, and within pain, there can be joy."

Darach clasped Brice's hand tightly in his. "I know we've talked about this but... Did what he did to you make you feel good? Did it bring you joy, or peace, or something? Because if that's what you need..." Brice removed his hand from Darach's grasp and raised it to Darach's mouth.

"For a while, I thought he brought me joy, but I told you, the more I researched BDSM and the lifestyle, the more I discovered it wasn't the case. I wanted to be punished for what happened to Sadie, and I craved the pain to block out everything else. I fooled myself into thinking Tommy cared for me, but in truth, he didn't. I had no real say in what he did to me — no safe words. Although I consented, there was nothing consensual about what we did. He was a sadist who simply liked to control people and hurt them. My head was so muddled, I didn't see the situation properly and I thought I owed him. He didn't take care of me after he'd done like a good Dom should. He hit me and fucked me then left me alone. I treated my wounds as best I could."

Darach's eyes filled with tears and he pulled Brice closer. "I'm so sorry," he said. "So sorry you had to go through all of —"

"Don't be sorry, Darach. What he did — what I let him do — had nothing to do with you. Pain gave me somewhere to hide and a reason to cry. I couldn't cry for her, you see, but alone in my bed, after he'd left, the tears would come. I don't need to cry anymore. Alisha helped me to see things more clearly, helped me to take control of myself. If I were to choose pain now, I would choose it for the right reasons."

Brice paused for a moment and Darach tensed, wondering what was coming next. Were there more revelations? Brice stroked his fingers down Darach's arm, making him shiver.

"Have you ever let anyone control you, Darach? Let yourself be tied up or blindfolded? Had a ball gag in your mouth, or plugs in your ears, and simply let yourself be touched — let yourself feel? Sensory deprivation can be such a turn-on."

Darach shivered again, not understanding why — fear or interest? — he wasn't sure. "Mitch handcuffed me to the bed once, but nothing else."

"You have to trust the other person. Alisha made me do research to show me how such relationships should work. I learned a lot. I never truly trusted Tommy. I let him tie me up, but all he wanted was to see and hear my pain. You, I trust. I know the power would be mine."

Darach felt every hair on his body rise as Brice lightly skimmed his chest and stomach with his fingers until his hand came to rest on Darach's hardening cock.

"Oh, God," Darach whispered as Brice wrapped his fingers around his shaft and began to move slowly up and down.

"I don't want you to see me as someone who has to be saved, either from others or from myself. I know who I am and what I've been. I'm not the same person anymore. I may not have working legs. I may be in a chair, but I'm not helpless, and even after everything that's happened, I won't be treated like a victim. I don't want a Superman who wears his underpants on top. I need a lover, a partner. There's only one Princess around here, and she's furry and likes to catch mice."

Darach laid a hand over Brice's and stopped his stroking. "Is that how you think I see you?"

"Don't you? Everyone else does. I've seen the way people stare at me when I'm in my chair — the poor cripple. And now I feel totally exposed. I may as well be naked out there. Now people know everything about my life, every little tawdry detail, so it's worse. I've seen the swift glances and the stares. People have even moved their children to the other side of the road, as if I'm contagious or something. It was bad enough when it was the chair, or the hair and tattoos, but now they know I'm a gay ex-rent boy, with a murdered sister, prostitute mother and abusive ex-boyfriend who had his fingers in more dubious pies than the woman in *Sweeney Todd*. They're either scared of me or pity me and see me as an unfortunate victim."

"Jesus, Brice. I think you're the strongest man I've ever met. You looked after your sister and mother. You made your choices, maybe not always the right ones for the right reasons, but you did what you could. You gave evidence against the gang. I don't see you as a victim. You saved yourself, Brice. You didn't die when they beat you up. You fought to survive. You reinvented yourself, and even down the well, you didn't give up. You're the hero, not me. You even put the tracker on the chair. You're so strong. I worry I'm not enough for you."

Brice gave a low chuckle in the darkness. "Shut up, you silly man. You're more than enough for me. When you look at me, I don't see pity. When you fucked me, it was perfect. You fucked me, the person, not just my body. And when I fucked you, being inside you, I've never known anything like it. Seeing you come, feeling my cock so deep within you. You are the only person I've ever… The connection between us. I want it forever. I want to be able to fuck you with nothing between us. To finally be able to trust someone."

Darach's cock sprang up. "Oh, God."

Brice grabbed his hand and placed it on his own erection. "See what you do to me, Darach McNaughton? Someday I want to be bare inside you, but for now, why don't you scoot over here and let me show you how much I want you, how much I love you and how much I trust you."

Darach didn't need asking twice. He reached over and grabbed a condom and lube from the drawer. He too couldn't wait until they could do this bare. Straddling Brice, he prepared himself, sheathed Brice's cock in the condom then lowered himself until Brice was buried deep within him. He leaned over and kissed his lover, sucking and biting his lower lip, kissing down his throat and chest, licking and sucking each nipple. Brice's upper body rose under his touch. He thrilled at every groan, every hiss of pleasure Brice made, finally taking his own cock in his hand until he came, shouting Brice's name, over his tattooed chest with the warmth of Brice's climax filling his insides. It was perfect. He never wanted to lose this man. Even in the dark, he could see the tears shining in Brice's eyes.

"I love you so much," he said. "I want us to work. What's happened has shown me that you have to grab happiness when you find it."

Brice smiled at him. "Well, you won't get any argument here. Now, we both need to get to sleep. I have a new website to construct in the morning and you've a sheep rustler to find."

Darach grinned before moving. They'd had too much extraordinary lately. Tomorrow's plans sounded absolutely perfect to him.

Epilogue

Nearly a year later

"Oh, my God. Stop fussing. You are such a wimp."

"I didn't expect it to hurt so much. It's all right for you, you're used to the pain." Darach jerked his head up and away from examining his chest. "Sorry, I meant you've had way more tattoos than me, not..."

Brice clasped his hand. "You're worrying too much again. I thought we'd moved past pussy-footing around what we say to each other. Come on, we're here to celebrate the end of the court case and your birthday because we didn't get to last year. I intend to enjoy this evening – dinner, a show and you ravishing me."

Darach grinned then hugged Brice. "You did so well in the witness box. Those bastards will be there a long time, and the gang has been broken up. Do you think your mum will stay in rehab?"

"I've no idea." It hadn't been easy seeing her again. She'd been so thin, chain-smoking and drinking herself to death. At least she'd managed to stay off the harder drugs. Darach had found her a program and she'd agreed to go. "But I hope so. I told her I'd keep in contact. Only time will tell." He gazed around the room.

"This hotel is lovely. I always forget Aberdeen has a beach." He wheeled himself to the window and pulled back the net curtain. "The room has a gorgeous view as well."

"It certainly does."

Brice turned and smiled at Darach. "We don't have time, so get that smirk off your face. Sex after the show, not before."

"But I might be too tired by then. I am thirty-one today. It'll soon be early to bed with a mug of cocoa for me. You'd better make the most of me while I'm still able to perform." He leaned back on the bed, his chest still bare from where he'd been examining the tattoo, hand on his crotch and legs apart. Brice wheeled himself forward until he was between Darach's knees. Darach continued to rub himself.

"You are a tease, Darach McNaughton, but it isn't going to work." Brice began to undress, slowly undoing each shirt button then wriggling out of his jeans and briefs. He knew Darach was watching his every move, but before he could reach out and touch, Brice wheeled back and moved toward the bathroom. He glanced backward.

"Perhaps you'd like to give me a hand in the shower," he said.

Darach didn't need asking twice. He removed the rest of his clothes and followed Brice into the bathroom, grinning from ear to ear.

* * * *

"You were right about the food here. I'm surprised you can push me, I've eaten so much. It makes a change to get so many vegetarian choices on a menu. Maybe I'll manage to get you to give up meat after all."

"No chance," Darach said, grinning. "I like the feel of meat in my mouth." He put the chair into position, and Brice reached down to put on the brake.

"At least we get a decent view from here. Not every theater is as thoughtful about where they position their wheelchair friendly spaces and you can sit next to me. I've been looking forward to seeing this show."

"I've only one thing to ask. Promise me I won't have to listen to you singing *Defying Gravity* for days."

"You're jealous I have a wonderful singing voice and you don't. The Moray Choir was so pleased to have me join them."

Darach had suggested it to Maggie when he'd overheard Brice singing to himself one day, his tenor voice soaring through a rendition of *Let It Go* that brought tears to Darach's eyes. Maggie had been a member of the local choral society for years and had clapped her hands with glee when Brice sang for her. After several performances, including Brice singing solo, Darach had loved the way Brice had blossomed, and with his business doing well and his making new friends, everything seemed rosy. The only blot on his horizon was his mother, but they would deal with her as they had with everything else—together.

People began to flood into the auditorium. The performance was sold out. By the time the curtain rose, Brice was brimming over with excitement and already humming the songs with his hand firmly wrapped around Darach's.

The show was as magnificent as they'd hoped it would be and Brice had indeed sung every one of the songs on the journey home. Even the dour taxi driver had cracked a smile, especially when Darach had handed over a large tip when they'd arrived at the hotel.

"Champagne?" Brice questioned, staring at the bottle in the cooler with two glasses next to it.

"It is my birthday," Darach said, popping the cork and pouring a glass of the fizzy liquid for both of them. He handed one to Brice.

"I wanted to tell you how proud I am of you and how much you've achieved over the last year. I've never met anyone as strong as you are. You've set up your website and Davy and Jason can't get enough of your tiles. Your paintings and pottery are selling well. You're singing in a choir and also working with students in the local schools."

"I'm not sure I'm ever going to feel comfortable on a horse, though."

"Well, you can't be good at everything." Darach clinked their glasses together.

"To us," he said.

"To us," Brice replied. "And happy birthday, old man."

Darach bent down and scooped Brice out of his chair, plonking him down on the bed.

"Be careful, I'm spilling champagne," Brice warned.

"Hmm, maybe I could lick it from your body." Brice raised his eyebrows and a few minutes later, they both lay naked with Brice in Darach's arms.

"How's the tattoo now?" Brice asked.

"Not so sore and yours?"

"Mine is fine. I'm used to it. This one is tiny compared to most of the others."

"Why did you leave a space there?" he asked, knowing the answer. He simply wanted to hear Brice say the words.

"You are such a soppy idiot. You know I left the space over my heart until someone claimed it, and that person is you. I love you, Darach McNaughton."

"I don't think I'll ever get tired of hearing you say it." He gazed at his own matching tattoo in the same position. "I've never even heard of a heliotrope before you mentioned it."

Brice gazed up at him. "It symbolizes eternal love. Now who's being soppy? I sound soppy, don't I?"

"You do, but I'm coping." Darach leaned forward and kissed Brice, tasting the champagne on his lips. Brice wrapped his arm around him, pulling them closer, but Darach managed to slip his hand between them and take them both into his grasp. Brice jerked in response then groaned as Darach continued rubbing, spreading their pre-cum over them both.

"Look at me," he said, his voice low with desire. "I want to see you come with me."

"Oh hell, yes, feels so good. I love your big hands."

Darach continued stroking while their breathing became louder and more labored. "Come with me," he whispered.

Brice's eyes were now almost black with desire. He raked his nails down Darach's back hard enough to leave marks. Darach moved his head, kissed Brice and plunged his tongue in his mouth as they climaxed, sending hot liquid between them. Finally, needing more air, he pulled back.

"That was…"

"Intense," Brice supplied.

For a while Darach stared at the ceiling, breathing hard, while Brice repositioned his head on his chest and lifted Darach's hand to his mouth to suck and lick his fingers. "I love how we taste," he said. "We go so well together."

Darach reached under the pillow and found the small box he'd placed there earlier in the evening. "I'm glad you think so because I've something to ask you."

Brice's eyes widened when he caught sight of the box. "Brice Drummond, I love you so much and I don't want to be without you. Now that the law has changed, I'd be honored if you'd marry me." He opened the box to reveal the gold ring with three diamonds. "The stones are supposed to represent the past, present and future," he said.

Brice continued to stare without saying anything. A small stab of worry penetrated Darach's mind. *Oh, God. I've buggered this up. He doesn't want to marry me.*

"Stop worrying. I can hear those cogs from here. I'm shocked. I never thought anyone would ever… That I'd be able to… Marriage—bloody hell."

"I'm conscious you haven't answered me," Darach said quietly. "If you want more time to make a decision, I'll understand. Marriage is a big deal. I get—"

Brice placed a finger on his mouth. "Shut up, you idiot. Of course I want to marry you. I'm merely overwhelmed that you've asked." Darach wiped a tear away from Brice's eye.

"Don't cry," he said.

"I'm so happy," Brice replied. "This is going to sound so soppy, but you've no idea how happy you make me."

Darach slipped the ring on Brice's finger. "It's perfect," he said. "Like it's meant to be there."

Brice held his hand up, turning it to and fro. "I intend to buy you one as well. I want everyone to know you're mine."

"Oh, I'm yours all right," Darach said. "And I'm going to be yours forever."

A Bell Rings

Excerpt

Chapter One

Nine months later

Jack reached out and found nothing but space. Confused for a moment, he opened his eyes and stared at the emptiness on the other side of his king-size bed. Two thuds told him George and Fred had landed on the mattress. Seconds later, the meowing began, followed by four paws kneading his side, then George, as always, head-butting him. Before George could stick out a paw to swat his nose, Jack pulled himself into a sitting position and glanced at the clock—seven a.m.

"Boys, it's Saturday. Is a lie in too much to ask for?"

From the noises they were making it obviously was. Jack swung his feet over and sat on the edge of his bed, rubbing his eyes. The cats swirled around his legs.

"All right, give me a few minutes and I'll be with you. I have to pee and clean my teeth first."

Jack staggered to the bathroom. He stared, bleary eyed, at the face in the mirror, which currently sported too much stubble. He'd shave later. His dark hair grew quickly, so he didn't want a five o'clock shadow forming by the time he reached the restaurant. Whatever Kay said about beards being sexy, he liked to be clean-shaven, neat and tidy, just like his flat with everything in the right place. He splashed his face with cold water in the hope he'd feel more awake — he didn't.

Still wearing his shorts and a T-shirt, Jack dragged himself through to the kitchen. The cats sat waiting next to their bowls, meowing as if they hadn't eaten for days. He removed two pouches from the box and filled each bowl before topping up their biscuits and water. Next he sifted the litter tray.

"I don't know how I cope with such a glamorous life. Next time I'm coming back as a spoiled cat."

Tea made and cereal and milk poured, Jack opened his laptop to check the news. An hour or so later, his mobile rang — Kay.

"Hey, Jack, you're up, then?"

"I might be lying naked in bed with the woman of my dreams for all you know."

"Yeah, yeah. You have to go out to find one first, and you've practically achieved hermit status. Just because I moved out doesn't mean it's the end of your social life."

Jack leaned his head onto one hand to prop himself up. "I'm beginning to think I'll never find the right person. Am I too picky, or what? Come on, you're a woman, help me."

He heard Kay sigh on the other end of the phone. "You are a wonderful human being, Jack Hastings, and if I swang — or is that swung? — in your direction, I'd have climbed all over you by now. You need to get out more, so don't you dare tell me you're going to dodge tonight. It's been thirteen years since we first met at university, and we need to celebrate. We haven't seen the others in like forever."

Jack thought back to the house they'd shared. There had been five of them – the sixth bedroom had never been occupied – him and Kay, Adam, Ewan and Peri. Adam had moved to New Zealand straight after graduating, so this would be the first time the five of them had been together since then.

"I'm looking forward to it," he said. "Even though I'll be the saddo by himself." He shivered. Something about the statement sounded wrong. Maybe Kay was right. He spent too much time by himself. The cats meowed from somewhere in the flat. He had no idea why he'd ended up taking in the two ginger kittens, but at least they were company for him. He sighed again. Time to get dressed and do the weekly shopping before visiting the barber. Even if he was the only single one among his old friends, he intended to look his best tonight.

* * * *

Several hours later, Jack pushed through the door to the restaurant, early as always. He strolled to the bar, ordered a beer and perched on a stool to wait for the others to arrive. In his cream chinos and white cotton shirt, he'd dressed to suit the weather, knowing the Indian summer would mean a warm room full of people. While waiting, he gazed around the space. The restaurant had an early-bird deal so many of the tables were already occupied by families, women in their floaty summer dresses, men in T-shirts and jeans, young children dressed in all sorts of outfits and colors. Papa Luigi's encouraged families to bring their children, and everyone appeared to be on their best behavior. He glanced up when the door opened. A woman in a bright red dress grinned at him – Peri. He rose from his stool and hugged her when she arrived at the bar.

"Jack, it's so good to see you. I can't believe it's been so long—five years. Where did the time go?" Peri had moved north to teach in Sheffield after graduating.

"I've no idea," Jack said. "Can I get you a drink?"

"A large glass of white, please. You're looking good, Jack. So tell me what's been happening in your life since we last met."

"Nothing much to be honest. Work is the same as always. Kay's moved out to live with Rachel, leaving me on my own, except for the cats." Hell, he did sound sad. "What about you? I expected Josh to be with you."

She stiffened and he knew he'd hit a raw nerve. "Let's say Josh and I are no more as of three months ago. He decided shagging his boss might get him promoted. Bastard told her we had an arrangement. The good thing is that I don't think she was right impressed with his performance as he didn't get the promotion after all." She drank at least half of the large glass in one go. "But enough of me. Anyone special in your life?"

Jack opened his mouth and nearly said yes. What the hell? Why would his brain even think that? This was the second time he'd had the same thought today, like there was something he couldn't quite recall. "No, no one special. I guess I'm not husband material."

Before the conversation could nosedive any further, the door opened and Kay entered with Rachel. Behind them followed Ewan and his wife, Natalie—more hugging and catching up. Ewan was a vet and Natalie a doctor, both with practices in North London. Ewan had stayed in the capital rather than returning to his native Edinburgh, but retained both his Scottish accent and his bright red hair.

"So, only Adam and his boyfriend to arrive now," Jack said. "Who'd have thought it? He kept that quiet at university."

"Maybe he didn't get it, then," Kay said. "Not everyone realizes their sexuality when they're young. Sometimes it takes someone special to make them see the truth."

Jack shivered once more, as if someone had walked over

his grave.

"Maybe Jack and I should try jumping the fence," Peri said, laughing. She nudged Jack. "What about it, Jack? Do you think you could fancy a bloke?"

Before he managed an answer, Kay whooped with delight as two men entered the restaurant. Jack recognized Adam immediately. He stood six feet tall, with blond hair and blue eyes, dressed casually in jeans and a T-shirt, but it wasn't his old friend who caught Jack's eye, it was the man with him. Adam's partner, Ross, stood even taller. Dressed in jeans and a plaid shirt, an ax wouldn't have looked out of place in his hands. Bearded, with dark hair and the shoulders of a swimmer, this man had a confidence and presence that Jack envied. He found himself scanning Ross from head to toe, taking in every inch of his body. When his cock stirred in response, Jack became even more confused. Had Peri been right? Was he, at thirty, suddenly interested in men? Instinctively, he put his hands in front of his trousers.

Adam hugged everyone then introduced his partner. "Everyone, this is Ross. I've filled him in on all of you. Now, what are we all drinking?"

Kay asked for the menus and they made their choices. Jack listened as the others talked about their families and jobs. He didn't say much, but then he didn't have much to add. He'd been doing the same job with the same bank since graduating. He visited his parents on weekends, and he hadn't had a proper date for longer than he could remember. Lately, he'd been less inclined to bother.

A waitress told them their starters were ready and they sat at a table near the back of the room. Fortunately, the restaurant had air conditioning, so it wasn't uncomfortably warm.

Jack continued to listen while his friends reminisced about their time in university, only half aware of their words until Kay nudged him.

"Jack, are you all right? You've been quiet tonight." She kept her voice low, talking only to him.

"Sorry, I'm feeling out of sorts. The flat is lonely since you left. I need to advertise for someone to share with, but I don't want just anyone. I might try putting a notice on the board at work. What do you think?"

"I agree you need to find someone to share with. I'm worried about you, Jack. And you should get out more. You won't find love stuck at home, although I suppose you could try one of those online dating sites."

Neither of them had noticed everyone else had stopped talking. Peri leaned over. "I'm on one of those. It's so hard to find a decent bloke these days." She turned to gaze at Adam and Ross. "So how did you two meet?"

Adam grinned. "I'm not sure you'll believe me, but Ross is a volunteer lifeguard. I got cramp while swimming and he rescued me — saved my life and everything."

"So from that moment onward, I had to take care of him and we're still together after five years." Ross put his arm around Adam's shoulder and kissed his cheek.

Jack had a sudden urge to get out of there. A great cavity had opened in his chest. Unconsciously, he raised his hand to check. His heart ached. Confused, he stared at the table's woodgrain in an effort to hide his tears that were threatening to fall. Unable to face the group any longer, he stood. "I'm off to the loo."

Once in the men's room, he stared at himself in the mirror. He threw cold water over his face. "For God's sake, get a grip. What the hell is the matter with you?" He turned, half expecting someone to be there glancing over his shoulder, but the room was empty. Something Ross had said sounded so familiar, but he had no idea why. He relieved himself then returned to the table, where they were discussing their first trip to Brighton and the infamous pub crawl.

"We slept on the beach, even though Jack lived ten minutes away, and nearly got arrested," Kay explained to Rachel and Ross.

Jack pulled a face. "That was because you and Peri insisted on taking your clothes off to go skinny dipping."

"The police officer had no idea where to put his helmet," Peri said, giggling at the memory.

"The police officer was *my* uncle, and I had a lot of explaining to do," Jack said.

Ross grinned at Adam. "So how come you kept your clothes on? Even in cold water you've nothing to worry about." Adam's face flushed.

"He was practically passed out by that stage," Kay said. "Total lightweight — unable to handle his cider — and these two were too chicken."

Ross grinned and affectionately muzzed Adam's hair. "He's still a lightweight in the beer department."

Adam put his hands on his hips. "I thought I was cute when tipsy. That's what you always tell me, or is that merely a way to get in my pants?"

"As I remember, there's plenty there," Ewan added. "He may have been shy on the beach, but the number of times I met him naked on the landing, even though we begged him to wear something in bed…"

"Says the man with the pregnant wife," Adam retorted. "Obviously nothing wrong with your equipment either."

Jack listened to more stories from their youth. He gazed at photo after photo of Ewan and Natalie's daughter and the views from Ross and Adam's house. Peri related several incidents from her teaching career. The more he listened, the more Jack realized how lonely he'd become — and how bored. He was a computer nerd who'd worked and lived in the same place forever. Truly, he had no life.

"I'm thinking of advertising for someone to share the flat with me now that Kay has abandoned me," he said.

"We have a new vet starting in a few weeks at the practice who's been searching for somewhere," Ewan replied. "I'm sure Fred and George would love him. His name is Raz Slade."

"Interesting name," Kay said. "He sounds ideal."

"Possibly," Jack replied. The name made him feel strangely uneasy. "But I don't know anything about him.

What if we don't get on?"

"He's lovely," Natalie said. "And very handsome. Ewan brought him to ours for dinner, and Lola loved him. He's our age as well, tall with dark blonde hair and the bluest eyes. He has this aura around him. You know how nervous Rex is around new people. He was all over Raz like a rash, trying to sit in his lap, which isn't easy when you're a large boxer dog. He obeyed every command Raz gave, like he had some sort of animal magic. Lola was the same. She's been asking after him ever since. He'd make a great flatmate for you, and he can cook. Why don't we give him your number and you can meet up? He's moving from the back of beyond somewhere up north. We'd agreed to put him up until he found somewhere, but your place would be ideal."

He did need someone to contribute toward the mortgage. "Okay, give him my number and we'll meet, although I'm not promising. Should I be aware of anything else?"

Ewan grinned. "He's gay, but that won't be a problem, will it?"

More books from
Alexa Milne

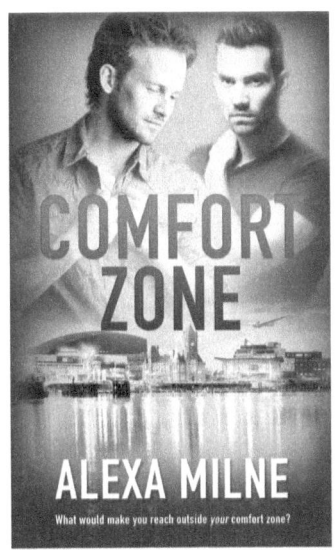

What would make you reach outside your comfort zone?

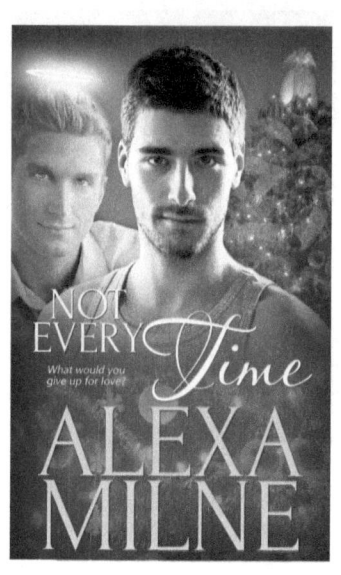

What would you give up for love?

Sometimes keeping hold of love is just as hard as finding it.

An act of kindness is never wasted.

About the Author

Alexa Milne

Originally from South Wales, Alexa has lived for over thirty years in the North West of England. Now retired, after a long career in teaching, she devotes her time to her obsessions.

Alexa began writing when her favourite character was killed in her favourite show. After producing a lot of fanfiction she ventured into original writing.

She is currently owned by a mad cat and spends her time writing about the men in her head, watching her favourite television programmes and usually crying over her favourite football team.

Alexa Milne loves to hear from readers. You can find contact information, website details and an author profile page at https://www.pride-publishing.com/